Casey—

Man—

dont eat

the black!

73

*Scandalabra*
a collection of poetry & prose

Cষ

by Derrick C. Brown

Write Bloody Publishing
*America's Independent Press*

Long Beach, CA

WRITEBLOODY.COM

Brown, Derrick C.
2ⁿᵈ edition.
ISBN: 978-0-978998-96-7

Interior Layout by Lea C. Deschenes
Cover Designed by Matt Maust, Josh Grieve & Bill Jonas
Photos by Matt Wignall
Proofread by Cora J. Duffy
Text Reset by Loulu Losorelli
Type set in Bergamo from www.theleagueofmoveabletype.com

Special thanks to Lightning Bolt Donor, Weston Renoud

Printed in Tennessee, USA

Write Bloody Publishing
Long Beach, CA
Support Independent Presses
writebloody.com

To contact the author, send an email to writebloody@gmail.com

*for President Jimmy Carter*

# SCANDALABRA

*For Andy Buell*
*True Champion of Poetic Terrorism*

# SCANDALABRA

# COTTON IN THE AIR

Your polished back is arched like Saint Louis.

I can see your fingers pushing into the bricks
when I lift your hair
to smell October drain from your neck.

You are cotton caught in the air.
I am unfurling laces in your body.

I move on you steady like a fleet of ships pushing ice.
I want to break it all.

Your tank top strap slips down the huh-huh-huh of your shoulder
and I will not strain meaning from this.

I am waltzing a wrecking ball.
I am wading in the dark felt Tijuana paintings of your hair.
I am molting my bed clothes, uncoiling towards Sahara.

All I want to do is hot lust you into dead sweat.
To watch your legs, those bent sickles,
to watch them shake
like poisoned wrens.

I am gnashed and dazzled.
Smother me in the exhausted thrust of your yes . . .
      wet as all exploding Laundromats.

May I be the image you turn to
when you are heaving alone,
burning like Halloween in Detroit?

I am breathing up your legssssspitting at the hiding nightingale.

Drift your breasts into my mouth
and I will be that doped up, spinning victrola singing:

La la la la la la.

I want to make love to you while you're wearing figure skates
until the hardwood floors are toothpicks.
I want to kiss your throat in a dressing room with my hands
bound around the slow song in your voice.

I don't care if you made that dress,
hippie.
I will shred it until you look deserted.

You're as restless as a New Orleans graveyard in a storm
with the coffins boiling up to the surface.

That's all this writing is. You are across from me and the soup is cooking.

I sit up all night listening to your dental records.

I will teach you of exorcism and screw the hell out of your limbs.

I carry your steam in my mouth.

Daydreaming of the evening of loud struggle.
Call my name—I will cascade like a suicide.
I will fall upon you like a box of fluorescent bulbs
dropped from a five-story building.

I will do anything you ask …
unless I have been drinking; then it is opposite day.

I can't believe you can sleep through all this.

Chunks of brick in your fingernails.
Mortar on your pillow.
A bomb shelter
sketched on your skirt.

It says Safe.

# PATIENCE

I cannot love you until you can love our beautiful waitress
in the simple way that I do.

# COLLIDE ESCAPE

When you drop something in the night
you should wait and recover it
in the morning when you're sober.

We will find the turquoise ring
that clutched the mud and grass
as I ripped your fancy jeans
down to your soft calves.

Can you sing while swimming?

The night rain beaded upon your skinny spine.
If you were drunk, I didn't know.
I was drunk.

Your tongue was blossoming into Lavatera, Lily, Cannas,
pronouncing your kiss, delicate,clean and bending wild.

Your eyes brewed hot enough
to melt the day's black resin from me.
I haven't felt glad in a long time.

I have swam in the wrong rivers.
Wet clothes everywhere.
I have made love into a messy room.

Can you sing into the sensational tangle?

Can you sing low frequency sonar?
Sing me the dawn like an AM radio?

I am suspended in the cinema of that moment

next to the house
where I needed you.
How we danced the Dirt Collapse.

Fathoms under fathoms,
I laid heavy upon you.

Can you sing me a fix?

Tell me you are more than on my side,
you are the weapon on my side.
I can say exactly what I mean
when armed and stupid.

Rest under the valley of the shadow of my gut.
Unsentimental kissing.
Our bodies gushing, strangers victorious.

Pyrokinetic honeysuckle, let's boycott the hocus-pocus.
I know you.
Aren't you the one snarling in all the family photos?
Are you the one crackling voltage from the yellow eggs? Yes?
Then you are the pearl I steal. Tell me about your sand.

It is rare to start recalling a moment while you're in it.

"I'm going to remember this now, cause I want to recall it in hi-res."

Your eyes leaving, a kaleidoscope of collide and escape.

If no one else finds the means to patiently adore you,
navigate back to me by the map of fallen stars.

Jewelry lost in a large wet lawn.

Some nights, love rises back to me
like an escalator fragrance.
It sings but isn't there. I hear it.

# THE BEST PICKUP LINE IS HOWLING

The best thing to say to an unknown woman when leaving a place is
"You and I are going to kiss someday."

I used to say, "You don't know me. So, when are we gonna make out?"
Some girls would take a long time, hemming and hawing,
thinking about what they had planned Thursday,
a year from not now.

The only response to
"You and I are going to kiss someday."
is
*Okay* or *No, thank you* or sudden howling.

When this happens, you should say...
"Sadly for both of us, it doesn't even matter if you want to."

# Banana Mandible

The trash is spread all over the living room floor
like the last days of the carnival.

I lie there, lost among it.

I see her weeping by the record player,
weeping out like the needle.

In those last days of us,
she cried all the time like an open mic.

I stare in the mirror at the place on my body
where her mouth last was. I can't recall the date.
I miss how her body felt like a mooring.
Someone who waited like a hospital.
Someone who kissed like it was critical.

Logic dead, guileless things.

O yeah, to unsophisticated love,
her young tongue, she was not afraid to say,
...we're fucked.

*Am I too ripe, too forlorn to remain? Am I the one?*

This was not the phrase that peeled me open and wasted me
like a banana left in the fridge
no one wants to eat, open or throw away.

The sabotage was done
long ago
some clear night
when my arms were a bad jacket around her.
The skin, smooth as fifty-dollar Lynchburg whiskey.
It's a dry town.
I fell asleep when she asked
how I felt about her.

Repeating the question into the back of my head,
Tall Love,
thought I was finally out of fancy language.
I dreamt quick.

She left before I woke.
If she could have only seen the world she slipped me off into.
Perfect sleep and honest silence.

Her sentence, undoing my pulse,
lulling me in her pppoppies.

How do I feel about you?
My answer: snoring, luxury dreaming, running from cliffs and bouncing,
naked in school and unlearning your legs into winglets,
chasing the devil and choking him out,
the Emerald City, the heartless, the unbrave,
the small, the brain-dead, witches and all,
welcoming us as royalty.

I love you in sleep.

All your records are in the wrong jackets.

# VAGUE SUBJECT MATTER

Now she is asleep.

Every morning she wakes up after me.
The dawn, yawning long through drapes.
She knows I watch her slumber.
I sometimes kiss her arm and she just slings it up over her head
as if a gentleman mosquito was seducing her poorly.

She dozes down and holds like a sunken fishing vessel.
I put my ear to her chest and there are wind chimes and
the sound of diving boards.
In the evening, after TV dinners and cheap beer,
before we get into our large bed that I still owe 700 dollars on,
there is some talking over our books.
"Is everything going to be all right?" she mumbles, drifting off.
I always say no and kiss her on the forehead.
Her face is washed. Prettiest without the paint.
Even her pajamas are in Technicolor.

I am black and gray, my closet looks like a stage-hand's.
I bought a pair of shoes with some color in the sneakers.
I ain't so dark, babe.

She can't get it on unless she has tea and toast first.
I sometimes sing while making her tea and toast.
PG Tips, sauntering in rainbow sneakers
like a groggy gay pride parade.
Hum and she sleeps through the work alarm.
I lay on top of her.
She says, 'Ahhhh. Man weight'.
It's time to get up, darlin'.
'But I don't wanna go to…church."

We never go to church.

She finally cracks her sticks and gets ready.
I love how she dresses
like a bowl of flowers in a dive bar.

I like listening to her bare feet hurry around, clumsy scutter.
She calls me a dirty word and it means she loves me.
I kiss her and squeeze the avocado breast.

I can see those scenes still.

Now that she is gone, all poems shorten.

I wonder if I can sell a bed so big,
so full
of so many types of mornings.

# DIVING SCHOOL

A story about a deep sea diver
sounds like it isn't going to end well. Nothing happens
by the time this poem ends.

I met the diver man in London. He only feared one thing.
I don't know if I should tell you.

He spoke of weekly diving expeditions into the unsympathetic ocean.
Blue, cold, eastern Scotland. His wife would wait at home.
He mentioned her small waist, cinched tight in expensive clothes.
I thought of police zip ties.
I've never mentioned someone and first described their waist.

He would bring home salvage money, tales of fish that glowed,
wet towels, and love. All of his love that he knew of.
He said she was not satisfied. She wanted him near.

She missed him and he knew it. Rust.
Her heart was so heavy, it dropped into her leg
and she limped when she shopped for new uneven shoes.

He spoke of his dream of the black urchin,
sucking something bright out of his body.
He had five beers and confessed that he had to make a decision.

In the urchin dream
he could feel his need for oxygen pulling him further to the surface
and far from the quiet beauty below.
He was sure he would drown in the air.

He peeled his beer bottle label/swore he had tried to change,
change to keep them together.
He combed his hair, ironed his shirts for the cocktail parties,
went shopping for a laundry basket to match the bedspread.

But he kept dreaming of the thing at the bottom.
He dreamt of it every night after drinking water.
He started taking sleeping pills

so he could dream more.
He might have to sell his diving gear for more sleeping pills.

At the department store together,
she tried on some things pink and new.
He recalled her asking, "Can we afford all this, dear?"

Her blouse surrounded breasts.
He wanted to suck on them like revolvers
to blow some holes in his head,
to let all the junk and salt water dreams out.

I asked if he still cared for her.

Have you ever died when someone asked you
how many spoons would be perfect in a new silverware set?
So late in the game
he was sure
that this
woman was his best chance,
his last chance,
at keeping love,
a kind of it.
He would sacrifice it all.

A glass of water by the nightstand.
A wheezing increasing in his lungs.

He said the one thing he feared
was having one minute of air left in his tanks
when his heart kept demanding three.

# JAPANESE PAPER

1.
The girl with the engine-black painted nails and legal drinking age
who hates the dog dying in her purse
needs me.
The business loafers,
cold water fountain drippings on their shirt.
Dehydrated faces with deep woeful lines like
bathroom stall wall knife graffiti.
They need me.
The foreign faces in bad sandals and heavy smiles,
lost and smelling like high school locker rags.
They need me too.
You can spot all these smokers coming off the plane.
One hand with carry-on bag, the other balled tight
as a ballerina's hair bun.
In the summer, I sold lighters
at the end of the baggage claim for extra cash.
I stood with a sign that said, "The lighter at the end of the tunnel."

I scored them from security for the departing flights.
I would sell them for pure profit, pulling about 130 bucks a day.

Relieved smokers often told me they loved me.
I knew the imperfect desperate look,
the ragged and provoked look.
They needed me, my smokes.

2.
There was one woman. Margaret.
The faint lemon grove.
and basil in her hair, rosemary breath.
A face full of traveler's sheen, heading nowhere in particular,
just getting away.
I miss her.

My hands smell of butane and I miss her classic smoke.
I think of her when I am holding still.

So many years before
I was tearing through horndog streets,
walking like a machete
through the lush envy of other men.
She asked for a light.
Her words came like a pre-monsoon breeze trembling
across Japanese paper. "Hello, delicate," she said.
I followed Margaret.
How it started is not as sweet as what we came to be.

3.
We were in the dumbest seasonal love.

We were laughing merlot up,
throwing bottles into the rafters.
Wine narcotics dripping upon our skin,
desire hoarse,
an aurora parade,
the bodies astonished.
For Halloween, you dressed as Thanksgiving.
I dressed as an "in-flight movie"
and bored you into my arms.
One evening I said, Margaret, every day, strangers tell me they love me.
I know that they don't really love me; they love what I do.
I like the sound of it no matter the intention.
We've spent months together
and you have never said that you love me. I want to see what it does.
I want to see if I twitch.

She said, "I love what you do to me."
I love what you do, too, Margaret.
The best relationships
fade out
and you're not even sure
when it ended.

4.
Back in my sweet spot by the baggage carousel,
a pink suitcase emerges.
I stare at it for too long and now I see a vision of a plane,

mid-flight, splitting
like the black seam of her stun gun stockings:

luggage and lingerie fall to the earth,
children grab umbrellas
as the sky roars down high heels, slinky neckties and
panties, panties...
panties panties panties...
No one survives but everyone gets a short thrill.
I don't think about what they lost.
I think, there go my customers.
There go the people that kept me alive.
I wonder if, on certain doomed flights,
people get that tingle that something isn't right
before it crashes, but you hope you are wrong and close your eyes
and wait to see if the plane stops shaking.
I snap from the daydream.

5.
I see the escalator bringing travelers down to no-waiting party
and I am there with my box of colors and sign.

I look at the screen of arrivals
and I see Margaret's home phone,
her bra size, her birthday in the numbers.
A man with his tie flipped behind his neck lines up to buy a lighter and says,
"Oh, buddy, you just saved my life."

Two dollars, please.
"I am surprised no one busts ya. Selling back to people
something taken away from them is kinda strange, huh?"
I am restoring the balance.
"You savin' up for vacation?"
I am saving up to buy a plane ticket to Nowhere Special. Two dollars.
He says, "You have no idea how thankful I am for this."
I say, I have an idea.
He rummages for a minute,
checking to see which lighter has the most fuel in it until his eyes widen.
"Hey, this is my lighter. I bought it in Texas.
This is the lighter they made me get rid of. What a trip.

I drew my initials on the bottom. See. D.G. I can have it, right?"

Sure, but there is a resurrection fee.

"How much?"
Two dollars.
Bags and bags coming down the carousel,
Endless.
Some never get picked up.

# New Machines

You can make love in the Sears dressing rooms.
They don't want you to, but I say do it.

Ask the sales person when there will be no sale.
Do not go during a sale!
I am asking you to trust me on this.
Do not go during a sale!

Sales mean moms and moms mean bored mean kids.
Kids like to crawl around and sneak under dressing room stalls,
wondering which one their mommy went into
and you don't want to ruin a child's life with
the sight of your non-mom mild jungle.

Hold your hand over your lover's mouth.
Kiss fast, slick and dead-on, like new machine guns.
Kiss like you couldn't beat cancer.
Kiss like you need to try her on.
Kiss like Hawaii being born. Kiss like Tomorrowland is now.
Kiss like you're mad at the blood in her larynx, mad at her hungry
        mouth, mad for her blurring electrodynamic strut buggy thighs.
She will never forget the grip in your suspense.
You will never forget this muted fencing.
If you buy something on the way out,
you will feel like whores...
beautiful
knowing
whores.

Do not go during a sale!

# The Unlimited Noises of Silence

There is this older woman.
She falls upon me, gorgeous,
an avalanche of slave diamonds.

She has a problem with her eye. Maybe cataracts.
I have a problem with my ears. Artillery.
I bang into her.

Mountain goats, locking horns—over and over on the bed's cliff
and no one wins.

She has the noises of science.
Train noises bellow from her joints.
She is always departing.

Her legs lock around me as if she were about to fall
to her trapeze-death.

We are on the floor and I think of moral bullfighting
and your overuse of drugstore perfume.

There they go, those canary fingernails, chipped in nicotine,
pulling at my hips until she docks
her fat French tongue.

Some words drift in her mouth
and appear like dead birds in the shore break.
"I am dead without you."
I say, "You're dead anyways."

She rolls her pantyhose down until they look like ankle doughnuts
revealing legs like shipyard pliers.
She gives the necessary kiss.
It is snarly.

I say, "You kiss me like I'm the last."
She replies, "You might be."

My chambers hiss.
Her teeth get lost inside me like surgical weapons.
I spit out the window.
Now, the night feels loose.

"Fix me. Fix me with all your fingers."
I think she's winking at me.
The lights in here look like they could go out at any minute.

We have an AM radio with a broken antenna.
It plays all night
and we both miss somebody else.

# VALENTINE'S DAY IN DRESDEN

I feel as ridiculous as faith-based food,
directionless like rain in outer space
when you reach for me.

Don't unfurl vanilla fantastic at the black molasses.

Our love would be as dumb
as a bomb on a boomerang.

Dentists boycott your sweet kitty teeth.
Figs in your lips.
Let's not fall in love.
I am tired of stroking that cat.

Do not show me that you are
an observatory of wet hot bummers and boy germs.

Don't come to me all dressed-up in a peanut butter and
nightmare sandwich. I will not bite.
Your eyes as boring as a desert photograph,
your body, a nude model for bad hotel art.
Jealous as the unpublished, Naked as an open bar.
I know your type. I know your font. Wingdings!
Zapf Dingbats! Verdana…wide!
Comic Sans-sadness.

You're a European mess
rolling around in my favorite dress
a mouth full of hell
and a chest full of hell yes.

Big deal, your eyes are green and gray.
Shut off the night vision, ya creep.

You kissed me on the throat.
What is wrong with you?!
You know that's where I make my money!
You made my heart go cocaine Max Roach.
The rude rising noise.

Our sex is just going to be a constant bungled stumbling
into each other's gross.
It is going to be like throwing pasta against the wall
to see if we're done.
I know your favorite drink is casual tea.
Don't pour it on me.

Get me to the hospital, now!
I'll have to tell the doctors how good I was feeling that day
and beg them to operate
to get me back to poetry normal.

Speak sugar all you want.

I don't believe what you say
but
I appreciate your tone.
You are my start.

Rich people start wars. The poor become flowers.
You are dive-bomber hell-diver.
I am working class 1945, ready.

It must be Valentine's Day
in Dresden.

# CUPCAKE

My arms reach to you as a Joshua Tree
with a big fat chunk missing out of its chest.

Your hands are hatchets.
Singing metal into the birch of my bones.

You are a wailing concert of good sleaze.
Concu-com-bine unconquered.

I collapse into the negro night,
blacker and simpler
than a shaving kit bag.
Precision black.

I dare the streetlights to bend down more to touch me.
They risk electrocution and bulb implosion
by a man who is gutter volt waltzing,
who is finding his own electricity.
I'm lit like the flashlight I would attach to a string
and slowly drop from a roof at midnight on New Year's Eve.

I can imagine the future woman
that slips out of that slim, young carcass. Older you is better.
I am touching your hot control.
ABABBUPDOWNUPDOWNSTART. Free man.
I am under your trapezius with my hands and I am summer-whelmed.
Air typewriters play
hoping you will arrive as the soundtrack of cheap heels
strutting through the soft font
of my name.

Show up for porch beers in my nightmares.

Motorcycle with me across the skulls of nurses
who could not lobotomize our madness,
over the fossils of lovers who never broke a sweat.
I am roaring grizzly atonement.

You have never sinned.
You have never, ever sinned.

I meant what I said when I said
I will start a pub called LOVE
and when you walk inside
there is a sign that says, you are in love, you are in love, you are in love.
When you leave, it will say,
You're all out of love.
Please raise your voice when leaving.

I need you to work for tips.

We will pool our money for the road atlas wanderfest,
continue to screw in the bathrooms of wherever.

You will be photographed
by flashes of dawn,
strobing through cheap sheets.

Let's ride to Fall Creek Falls in Tennessee and abandon our skin.
I will take you there. You will shiver and ooze.
I will towel off your veins and sinew.
I will zip up your spine and you'll be ready for the great slow dance.
Slower.

You are in love. Somebody's got to be.
Break out the hatchets and cupcakes.
We are open for business.

# BEAUTY MARK OF THE BEAST AT MACH SIX

I am so alone.
I can only think about listing my name
in the phonebook.

Every ambulance singing
is singing for me.
When I am at the party
I find myself alone and sweating like a minister
who lies to his wife when he looks at her,
who cannot hold up under the weight
of the trust of an entire congregation.

I feel this when
she is out in the night,
pulled into that indigo magnet.

Soft loss chanting.
You were not that
beautiful, my league.

Listening to the kind of snow
that doesn't want to land,
the mass ivory quilt.

I am one of the drifting.
Those who have been outfucked,
dissed by nature.
We will warm as one.
Vanish.

I want to surge up from the mass like
the wasted body of the mayfly,
to take to the air for a moment,
die in the air once I can go no higher.

I see ravens mate.
I see them penetrate each other's blackness.

Come on, birds.
I'm next.

I stare at the mother's round stomach in the grocery store.
What a show off.

When I am alone and my skull is ripsaw,
I want to jump into the womb of any bonfire,
I want to leap into the ceiling fan head first
and see who wins.

Desire is on the couch with you, antlers and all.
You are too tired to mount it.

You can send someone compassion
in First-Class Mail
and if they can't accept it
or wear it like perfect pajamas,
it will return to you
and sit on your porch all beaten up.

If your affection grows in turbine gusts,
it will not meet them, it will pass through them like zephyr,
the hole will be tundra. You will be a piece of snow in it.

Everything is big when you are down.
Where are the bones of Goliath?
Some things are too big to bury.

I feared losing you,
not for the cost,
but because I heard
we become the things
we have lost.
She is held and kissed by a man with beautiful long hair.
You go for that kind
when you miss your mother.

She is gleaming with merchandise, she is laughed upon.
She was a large ruby moment.
She is now a place you can't touch.

She has turned into a thousand little rubies in his new hands.

I must let go of seeing her new beau
as only a style,
as something powdery that fades from the face.

He and I, we don't sing the same song
but we play the same instrument.

How strange to love a song
when you can't recall the melody.

# MEATLOAF

My mother is washing the dishes and singing
a song about someone dancing on the moon.
She stops to pat the globe of her stomach.
"So full."

I help her with the dirty meatloaf dishes and pass them from the table.
The gunk slides through the soap
and the green goo slips across her strong hands.

There is a flash of light every time she turns
her palm through the soap.

My mother has a small diamond
that she received on her wedding day.

It was given to her by my father,
as a symbol.

It was very affordable.

I always asked her why a diamond meant
that you loved someone?
Why not a brick, snail or wombat?

Why not give them a cat's brain to show them you are crazy about them?

Why not give someone a pair of handcuffs
to show the world that this person will be doing time with you forever?

Why not give them a trophy of a zombie lipstick to prove
that you will kiss their brains out forever?

There is dishwashing liquid in a brigade of bulging bubbles
and the 'tink spink' of moving plates and my mother is singing again.

To her, the diamond ring is a cheap, special reminder:
She says when she first saw the ring, it caught light
and shot it into her eye like fresh grapefruit.
She says my sister and I did that too.

The filthy forks sifted through her hands as the disposal burled:

"Gnrlwygnlrygnlrywy."

She stops singing and turns off the disposal.
Her face turns the color of the kitchen sink walls.

Water off.
She tosses through the plates.
She pulls out a rubber doodad to check the garbage disposal,
continues this for about ten minutes.

I wait for her to say it.
I can feel my face, ready to burst like a cloud.

"It's gone. I can't believe we were just talking about it and it's gone."
She pats my head and hands me a paper towel.

"It's okay, Mom. It's just a thing."

"Not really." She starts to weep a little. "Excuse me."

She goes to the bathroom to blow her nose,
returns, kisses my head and goes back to washing the dishes with me,
        scanning every bubble's gleam for the rock.

I roll my damp paper towel into a ring shape and give it to her.
"Ma, if we weren't blood, I'd marry you. And I'd stick around."
She replies, "That is sweet, Derrick. A little weird, but sweet,
        Derrick. I know what you're trying to say."
She grabs some tape so it would stay wrapped up.

I sneak outside to the neighbors' place,
steal her a brick from their garden.

When I come back in,
she smiles and begins to sing that song
of someone somewhere
dancing on the moon,
a song about a boy spinning in the dark
with one beam of light.

# FULL METAL NECKLACES
*(for Andrea Gibson)*

You are laughing up moths
bleeding in your boy pants
breathing your poems out like burning garlands.

Soon,
a woman from the audience,
full of woe and strange posture, is crying on you.

I watch your hands sheath themselves
into your safe back pockets.
You're not sure what to say or how to hold all of this woman.

I don't know what kind of advice
can make the anchors in the fan's neck
go away.

The woman is a girl.

When her crying slows,
your arms wrap around Girl
as if someone is going to steal her skin.

You hang there
like a constellation settling into its own black.
Looks like she is holding you up. She is.
A young girl slung around your neck,
snot and tears
staining your boring sweatshirt.

So many more to embrace. So many more sweatshirts to ruin.

We are necklaces, dipped in your voice-box, shining metal struggle,
crazed and heavy around you.
Your gay sweatshirt, a traveling canvas,
painted in the unfurling mess of us.

Your poems growl for a living because you hear the dying,
unsure of how to whisper.
I used to tell people poetry is hidden in everything. It isn't hiding.
It is waiting, just waiting for someone to call it on a Thursday night,
or ask it over for chili, or hold it tightly until it catches its breath.

# Barney Sheehan Lives Forever

Two tired Americans stumbled through the stone streets
of Limerick, Ireland.

Our money dissolved.

The books beat against our backs in our rucksacks,
heavy as the great mossy castles in the skyline.

The Irish breeze chased us into every pub.
We drank slowly until we forgot the chill.

My jacket
was lost,
floated away, downstream
drenched in Swiss river water,
British gasoline and German wine.

What black angel spent the night on guard
teeth chattering
eyeing my jacket
until she caught my faded head
and laid me in the cobbled gutter
and stripped it as payment?

In the morning bus, the fields raced us,
flared gold and would swing emerald light.
We had settled in desperate cities.

We were starving for new epic territory.
Beauty swallowed us in Ireland and Barney Sheehan,
a former jockey with hell in his veins and sainthood in his heart,
turned us into family.

We were living off the kindness of strangers,
drink tickets,
long embraces,
conversations of religion and death grazes.

He showed us the pride of Limerick
with bright energy in his vinegar/black beer tongue.

"Now boys, do ya want some eggs, boys?
Oh sure ya do, sit down and eat it up, go on, you know I ran for mayor once,
I woulda been absolutely fantastic, I would. Two votes!
Eat those eggs now! C'mon ya skinny little…
what do ya want to do boys, oh I'll tell you.
We're going to see the city is what we're going to do.
Now c'mon, you're not done eating, You know you're my boys…"

The streets of Limerick were coiled like a tired sea monster.
My pal Joel walked as fast as Chicago
and kept up with Barney's amazing pace better than I.
I walk slow in Polaroid.
I told them I may never ever see this place again
so I need to walk real slow.

Barney Sheehan took us to the cozy White House Pub
where the people listened as if poetry mattered and it did.

In the window, Barney had hung an Irish flag and next to it,
an American one.

"We're all the same. Everyone in America is Irish anyway.
You're home. Consider yourselves home, my boys."

The poetry and beer were hauling into everyone.
You could feel the words wedge right into people's chests.
This was Limerick,
far from the soft girls in Dublin that
danced with us in a boathouse until the yellow bolts came on,
piercing the thin skin of sky.
Charlie is the best name for a girl you will never see again.

A mesh of starlight fell across the island.
The streetlamps guided us through the tendrils of Limerick.
Cars whispered fast.
I was falling.

The soft hills, inhaling the night.
Morning dropped all over us.

Barney showed me my history in a Brown family crest
and something inside felt ancient for the first time.
I had never had a history until that moment.
To know that you are from somewhere very old
makes you belong to that soil,
your bones go solid.

The next day, I went to a river in a noon as overcast as wool.

A country with an arm spanning west
held me as still as the Lake of Innisfree.

The small tide came to me and loosened the soil.
My spirit.

Near the middle of the lake,
two swans,

one moving fast,
the other slow.

The drifting swan,
a glimmer in the wing,
sunlight brailed in its feathers.

We are treading.

I wondered about Barney
and what good words meant to him;
how they composed his life,
how he fell in love with writing
even though words leave him waving.
I looked at his handsome crags of skin,
his house of comfort and solitude
and I saw myself in his curious lake of graciousness.
I found this poem in his library:

## When You Are Old
*When you are old and grey and full of sleep,*
*And nodding by the fire, take down this book,*
*And slowly read, and dream of the soft look*
*Your eyes had once, and of their shadows deep;*

*How many loved your moments of glad grace,*
*And loved your beauty with love false or true,*
*But one man loved the pilgrim soul in you,*
*And loved the sorrows of your changing face;*

*And bending down beside the glowing bars,*
*Murmur, a little sadly, how Love fled*
*And paced upon the mountains overhead*
*And hid his face amid a crowd of stars.*

—YEATS

Barney,
I do not know when I will return to Ireland
to see your face in that silver crowd,
but I promise I will return
if you keep your promise
to live forever.

# POWER

For a reason,
it is hard to clean up blood
when it spills.

It tags the spot we were wounded in,
a flag, a theater curtain opening heavy,
the cinema spreading dark.
It doesn't want to go away,
it holds even the underside of our skin.

Maybe this is why, at the Rainbow Motel in Memphis,
they had to use a cutoff saw to break away
the large reddened concrete balcony piece
that Dr. King
breathed his spirit out on.

# BLAZING THE VALLEY IN PSALMS

Walking alone in the woods at night is
terror sound discovery.

Every crackus-fwish-clek of twigs
is a demonic rabbit sharpening switchblade teeth.

Every snap-pop in the dark
is a lusty python breaking a prairie dog's clavicle
and you're next.

Every simple rustle
is a man-tarantula regurgitating city brains.
Aren't you from the city?

In the morning,
in the burnt sienna of Ojai air
the paths are tossing me good music.

Hard sunlight
fumbles through dawn leaves.

The postal winds sleep
through their deliveries.

Cicadas and grasshoppers rewire the air ece-lec-tic-tric.

The rattlesnake has been grounded
for sticking his tongue out during dinner.

The tarantula is trying to find affordable pedicures.

I make my way to the place of meditation
and this is not something I usually do.
I fear hippies. I fear their free-wheelin' death traps.

Meditation seemed like something you'd do
if you owned a Subaru Forester and organicked
all the fun out of your life.

These days call for emergency cleansing.
I am an almost earthquake.

I sit with a ready heart and I try to cross my legs.
I am famously unlimber.
Feels like I'll crack.

I roll around in a weeble-wobble for ten minutes
trying to get my legs to learn impossible origami.
I ended up laying flat like a dead starfish.

I try to settle my breathing in the humidity
and right as I get close
a bug comes to whisper in my ear,
"Sssssss son of a bitch."

I am not Zen enough to not want them dead.
I want their tiny shit-eating children dead, too.
I move to get my brain resettled.

After two days here, I realize I have never had so much
fruit and granola in all my life.

Real fruit.
My body is confused.

My mind goes applauding up into the oaks.
The leaves' ragged voices flitter, "You're almost there."

Huh? I ain't close to anywhere.
Peace has a restraining order on me.
Peace is just the raise of two meaningless fingers in a tourist's lame photo.
I tell them that back in the real world…

There are mountains that have risen up against me.

There are rivers that are rising to swallow me.

There are winds that are whipping me out of my path, daily.

I am not sure whether to sit still
make camp
or quit.

There is death that I spoke into the walls of the valley
and the valley…welcomed it with gentleness.

Tonight I feel like joy is an ice pick,
I must go down in the garage and get.
The ice pick never comes to me.

Tonight I feel peace is a floodlight
that can either find me eventually
or I can run to it
as it signals out to me in the casual cover of night.

Spirit of pummeled rust, un-centered,
let my crooked song be a beautiful sound,
enlightened rough…not in an urn or a temple but
in a crock pot, a ghetto blaster or a pawn shop drum throne.

May this broken spirit drum away like a deaf child,
alert and pounding his heart out for a Love Colossus.

Gunmetal is the night.
A tarantula dances around the candle,
prim and without fear of burning alone.
I too burn alone.

My kind of sacred is a small toenail re-growing for no reason
or misapplied eye shadow for the "Ladies in their 80's" night out
or boners in front of nurses.

I get to say what is sacred or what is not.

The breeze cooks around me.

I travel upwards across a path that feels
like a row of deep breaths.

I slow in the heat.

I travel to the greatest oak.
I am empty-headed and lusty to shed my grief.
The swing is empty.
The hummingbird zazzes.

I tell the tree of my oncoming glorious collapse.
I speak of all the wasted effort
and the flappers' lips and the sorrow on stilts.

A psalm comes to me.
I watch it approach along the floor of the plains,
racing like a glowing cannonball,
blazing up the valley, smacking me in the jaw
and spreading into my blood.

It says:

To the rivers rising around you:
...spread out, arch upon it and speak life raft,
you will get to shore faster.
To the winds whipping talons against you:
...sail into its force,face first,and you will gain speed.

To the mountains rising above you:
you should say,..move.

You will say move.

# OVERDAZZLED IN AVALON

On the edge of the coast,
under the broken headlight of sunset,
we raised the sails of the Billie Ocean.

All four of them turned to catch the wide heaving of salted
Long Beach wind
bursting into the sheets of the small open seas yawl.

I lived on this ship and all of my books
would fall from the cabinets and shelves
depending on which way we were tacking.

Amelia Earhart and Houdini plastered to the cabin ceiling,
holding fast. Both lived lives in small spaces.

Spin the wooden wheel into the waves as the ocean rises,
as night lassoes down colts of radiance.

The wind becomes an eerie breeze,
a mistress in the ears.

The fish below think we are birds
and wish for flight.
They wonder how that much air
doesn't ever feel like too much.

Catalina Island from the Shoreline Marina in Long Beach
should be a five-hour sail.
It took us ten hours to arrive.

Why?

I keep trying things in my life
that might make me feel like more of a man
but end up
almost killing me.
When will I learn that a man
is just a tall horny baby?

The coast grows gray as a reaper's blade.
Death waits in the stale history behind us.

If you are surrounded by sea at night
with no coastline in sight
and the ocean, growing like a bad stomach,
tie yourself to the wheelhouse
and keep on.

It will feel like a nightmare when the wind picks up
and you can't tell where the waves are coming from.
That's the point.

Someone, after the journey, asked what sailors think about
with all that time alone and rocking. You think about:

Seasickness that feels like seventy-thousand simultaneous hangovers.

Engines burning out, diesel smell staining your body.

The wind falling asleep when you prayed to it.

Losing the anchor and seeing the chain vanish down like an eel into a cave.

You will cry and it won't stop you from ruining your propellers as
    you drift to the shore.

Tying off to another ship and having the teak shatter against a dock,
feeling that smash feeling in your fingernails.

The Sweet Pea dinghy sinking and laughing.

The unknown pleasure of a ten minute shower of hot water for a dollar fifty.

The fearless Garibaldi's of Avalon that move like confused treasure coins.

The seals that race your ship and win.

The rare Santa Ana winds fighting us on the way home.

Lips bleeding and face crystallized in salt
looking like bakers at war.

Shore House Café on Second Street.
It's not the best place to get a beer
but it is open late.
The waitress must have thought we were coke heads,
all bloody, white crusted and sunbeat.

"Well, we made it."
And that's it.

Horrible when you're in the trauma,
soon it's all a little memory at a party, a short sentence,
no matter how wonderfully terrible it was.

# THE PARANORMAL CHANNELS
# OF LONG BEACH

1.
The woman was big-boned and frantic dance shrieking.
The man pacing, yelling into his cell phone for God or an ambulance.
1:57 in the morning.
Easter.
The guard rail of the off-ramp wall was ripped apart.
I parked on the 6th Street exit from the 710 that leads
into downtown Long Beach.
Others were pointing down into the large reservoir below.
Someone had launched their car into it.
I couldn't find a way down there and I gave up.
I wonder what they said before they hit bottom.
I wonder why I automatically thought it was a couple.
I had pizza from a microwave.

2.
Last night, I heard three clear gunshots.
A man walked from the Mexican restaurant below my window,
his arm bleeding a great gush.
His girlfriend or wife was chasing him as he hobbled towards
oncoming traffic.
"Carlos, come back. Let me help you!"
"This is your fault!" he yelled.
She could've taken off her heels to catch him.

3.
There was blood and a syringe in the bathroom stall, last night.
Seventh and Pine. We all share one shower and four restroom stalls.
Someone put a paper plate with a kind of poem on it,
pasted it to the wall.
"Whoever is using needs to clean up their blood, their life. Thanx."

4.
Tonight, someone in a Camaro pulled in front of my tiny loft,
yelled at their girl and chucked a purse out of the car window
as she exited the muscle suite.
A gold necklace, mace, a pill bottle and cigarettes lay on the pavement.
If that is all you've got in your purse, then you are definitely ready for
     war, you can handle solo,
you can inspire every party.

5.
We would sleep on my bed raised by stilts,
staring out the window of our city's paranormal television.
Cop cars cut off a black BMW
and threw a Vietnamese guy onto their car.
I heard the words "attempted murder."
The girl got out, crying like a car wash.
They didn't cuff her. They told her to find a ride home.
He was yelling, "Don't tell them anything, babe, don't tell them anything."
By the way she was crying and reaching for him, I knew she loved him,
no matter who he had hurt, no matter how long he would be put away.

If you knew you had that, you could do anything.

# Ambien

They found daisies growing in Jonestown
where the bodies and grape punch
laid in the pavilion 30 years later.

Hyacinth Thrash, 76, was there that day of the massacre,
slept through it all,
saw her friends who left for heaven
and decided to live.

The feeling washing over her
as she tried to remember the dream
she had before waking to the sight
of everyone she loved, gone.

I want to sleep that hard tonight
with the world
convulsing around me.

# BEYOND THE CLEARING,
# A SOUNDER OF BOARS

Through the curtains of night oak,
into the clearing near the back of my house,
the sounder of boars returned.

Snouts along the ground
swaying like metal detectors.
Tusks, white as shards of new soap.
They advance, steadily,
creeping with blood stains on their chin fur,
plague in their hot breath,
surging slowly to my yard.

Sows grunt in cadence
as piglets swing their heads agreeing with the noise.
Stripes in their bristles emerge from the tree line
and soon in formation, they advance.

Hooves of the sounder crunch
through flakes of autumn like the boots
of a new search party.
I am surrounded.

They do this every year, in the same season.
At first I wondered if it was a friendly ritual...
they growled their mystery.
They waited in silence sending up rough grunts
and guttural howls, bellowing the awful melody,
haunting the mist.

As their black bodies filled my field, I became scared.
I wanted to kill them.
I do not love killing animals
as much as I love having killed animals. It's for food.
The meal is tastier than the hunt for certain men.

At first, I appeased them with acorns and candied pecans.
The third year, I moved on to confrontation.

I kept some spears in the coat closet behind the vacuum.
No gun. I drink too much to keep one near me when I begin to sink.
Some days I am bloated passionate.
Some days I am a brick in a pond. The gun would be a bad, loud joke.

When the long tooth boar began its mournful song,
I launched an attack.

The remaining spears I chucked were weak shots.
I launched the spears as fast as I could from my porch,
lobbing them in an arc for distance.
I scattered those bloody bristles.

My arms trembled from lack of nutrients.
They would not let me leave.

They returned in an hour
and the army of boars waited.

I did not know what they were waiting for.
—a meal?
—my home?
—warm blood?
—me?

Another year and I moved to giving them sacrifices.
Small turtles and a wristwatch placed in the clearing.
A box of photographs.
They would attack them in a shredding rage, but only when
the God of the boars moved his hoof, tapping it onto the ground.

There wasn't much more I wanted to offer them.
The few objects I did own were precious to me.

I offered a rabbit last year.
They dragged it from my porch,
impaled in the leader's tusks,
blood streaking my wooden planks.

I watched from the window
as the beasts ravaged it,
charging into each other like drugged rams
warring for the remnants of its body.
Sliding back beyond the clearing,
they marked my land with the hare's tragic red mess,
leaving the bits of its carcass to rot.

This year was different.
I had never seen an animal look resolute, maybe a bull.
They came and posed.
I turned on a floodlight.
Some were red as demons.
Some were black as Georgia molasses.
Some were glossed in sweat. Some tusks were three feet long,
swooped towards the pocked moon.

I held fast in my house for more days,
a hostage to the beasts.
The yelping infant boars were eager for something.
The God of the boars
stood in the center
while the others formed a tight disciplined circle.

I was running out of food.
I was weak.

The last of my tack was a half-skinned deer, a small buck
from the summer crossbow hunt.
I kept it in the garage freezer.

I carried its dead weight to the porch
as an offering and wished I had a phone that worked
or a big wife who could wrestle animals
or neighbors with the gumption to check up on me
or friends with guns.

I stood there behind the dead buck, desperate, alone,
caked in bits of ice and defrosting animal,
skinny as the spears jammed into the field.

I displayed the young meat for them.
The boars grunted and only the God boar stirred,
lifting his evil neck and holding his ground.
They all remained staring into me
with marbleized black olive eyes.
None approached.
I was exhausted.

"What do you want from me?"

Nothing.

"Do you want me to come with you?"

The long God boar surrounded by the others
patted a hoof at the ground.
They rose and spread like the red sea, a path to the God boar.

"Can I pack my things?"

The red boar snorted goop onto the soil.

"Can I write a letter?"

The God boar squatted onto his belly and the others followed as dominos.

I came back inside to tell whoever finds this:

I don't know if you should look for me.

If you do, I couldn't take any of my possessions.

I am probably beyond the clearing
through the oak
deep into the thick, lawless wild,
I packed nothing,
wandering
in a most beautiful ending.

# AFTER THE BACHELOR'S PARTY

Twenty-seven floors up in the Hilton, Las Vegas.
My buddy is getting married soon.
I'm beat and alone, kind of empty.
If someone wears their clothes to bed a lot,
it means something is wrong in their life.
I wore my clothes to bed.
I'm almost out of money.
I got enough for a sandwich tomorrow, one slot pull,
and a banana.
I eat bananas after I drink
hoping it will save me.

Room 2721.
The sun has dusted the mountainside.
Come home rust bucket sunset.

This city, a one-night stand that won't stop calling me,
an anthem of falling change,
the goofy mess of noise.

I like to stand around the glowing sadness,
that dumpy old sadness
sitting on every stool
all across this town.
They are waiting with a bucket full of nickels,
running down the clock,
drinking the classics,
forgetting to eat,
blowing the last of the government check,
calling it vacation.
Everyone is synced up to slot music
and perishes in unison.

I am no longer against it.
I have fallen
for the choke and chance of this pearled-up harlot.
Just having at least one chance feels good,

feels like it's all you will ever need.
That's why Southern people marry young.

I dressed up Joel like a knight for his bachelor party and wandered.
Strip clubs are too depressing and expensive.
We gamble nickels and sing in the streets.
Hollowed out like a watermelon,
I can still sing
and do failed keg stands on tiny beer cans.
I go back to the Hilton.
I love low television after a hot shower. I love the news.
I love watching it so long
you can hear the anchors struggle to rephrase the same story.

Someone was shot and the local station was there first.

This afternoon, the news was three boys.

No one saw anything.
In the sticks, gunshots explode
in a way so that no one can ever hear them. No one snitches.

My hair is wet after singing songs I hate in the shower
and my feet are sunburnt from
reading *For Whom The Bell Tolls* by the pool
and the sheets are cool
and three boys are dead.

I put on my shoes to see if that makes me want to go somewhere.
It sometimes works.
I walk to the window,
a reflection sags.

In the distance to my left,
the Stratosphere Hotel is dangling people over the ledge for coaster thrills.
I get the same feeling watching casino drunks kiss.
I'll head down there and write my way out of this bag.

I stand by the roulette table and the writing comes.
I am writing this feeling down because sometimes
I am a believer but a forgetter

and sometimes I look at all the things around me that
make want to kill all those beliefs in us
and say fuck it, today, I am going to nowhere. I am marrying this feeling.
Today I'm selling this loathing and cynical film score.

Today I'm gonna call the bomb squad and ask them to dismantle me.

Today I'm gonna talk about everything I am supposed to be ashamed
    to talk about.

Today I'm gonna beat off to the Song of Solomon.

Today I'm gonna throw this wine bottle into the river,
a piece of paper inside that says, "tell it like it is, not like it was, Bubba."

Today I'm gonna run naked through this casino and say, "I bet it all!"

Today I'm gonna pour some money I shouldn't be spending
into a machine that helps me get rid of all this future ash.

Today I'm gonna knock on your door and grab your ass
and drag you out to sea with me forever. Dress warm.

Today I drive with my love around my ankles and I'm gonna let you steer.

Today I am thrashing like an idiot.

Today I'm not gonna worry about when or if I will get married
or when the money will run out
or when I will be honest enough to make myself whole.

A hot shower. Three boys gone back to the ground. A banana.
All of it meshed together is living.
The sound of a casino everywhere.
You do not have to die inside.
Take off your clothes.
Crawl into bed.
Turn off the TV.
Call your friend.
Tell him you are happy for him,
and so thankful.

# BAD ARITHMETIC

you run a comb through your hair before you call her.
you start with, darlin',

she interrupts, says, sometimes.

you hang up.
you mess your hair
and head to a bar,
all gnarled up and greedy.

you feel his hands all over her, finding persimmons.

you are loaded.
you are swinging around in the air, the wild baseball bat,
a dance called emptying the cash register.

you thank her for the lease.
you remember that beauty
is a puddle that dries up when the sun comes out.
the day is warm.

sorrow is a song sung
with no harmony.
you can sing it well
the more you practice.

# Malibu Goes Home

The night has flipped and the bottom is burning.
The sewers are full of people, the aching sludge bluster.
The missiles are accelerating.
The government is trying to tighten the screw the wrong way
and we are stripped.
The curtains are open but the light plays in reverse.
We are in the belly of a chopper and
the chopper is still going down.
The billboards are getting heavy.
There are too many flags on too many graves.
California is on fire.
We head out to sea.
From one mile out,
Malibu blazes in fading bells of haze.
We leap from the ship and swim.
The water, freezing, full of life.
Seals rushing away from our death engines.
The smoke, yellow and raising over the tossing Pacific.
The whole sky changes to yield.
I laid on the bow next to you.
There were two sunsets in the smoke and horizon.
We sailed off into the first, leaving the second for the dead.
The bad wind moving,
pushed from the bagpipes of Santa Ana.
Malibu is clawing its way out of its Sunday clothes.
The heavens are full of Canada.
Mexico is rescuing the sun.
The United States is impenetrable.
It's all going down.

I do the splits
while the world crumbles into flames.

# OH COME NOW, FORCES OF NIGHT

Oh come now, forces of night.

Come against me.
Show me who I am,
for what I wished I was
has faded
like the tips of the Andes.

I can no longer lift my arms to the heavens.
I can no longer mar the one I long for.
The mast has snapped.
No ballast.
No chart.

Losing like this is
getting pulled away in the riptide,
the day after you lost your voice.
It is the way the moon gets smaller
for someone buried in the earth,
still alive.

Oh come now, forces of night.
I want to roar like a concentration camp revolt.
I want the volcano's incandescence
to drip through my words, through the floorboards in my choking brain.
I want the tar pits of loss to heave around me, to slurp my darkness out.
I want tendrils!
A robust clenching around you.
Blood suck,
tingles of ticks in your hair,
suck it out.

Oh come now, forces of night.
Don't turn me feverless,
I wanted what she could become, not what she was.
Her good flesh, chronicled in a panic novella.
I want her to think of me during lovemaking.

I want her to think of me shaving.
I want her to know they found licorice in Tut's tomb from 5,000 years ago
and the signs of it not being used show
we were wasting good things
on the dead.

All amateur comics,
have lame timing.

Here is a new condom that you opened,
for the lost smell of being safe
and wanted at the same time.

Her skin was taut gauze. A shroud around a thunder storm.

Oh come now, forces of night.
Send someone who doesn't undress everything cloaked in magic.
I'll give up a foggy passion in exchange for a simple lighthouse.

Oh come now, forces of night.
Blow me up like a basement in Palestine.
My anger was a mangled dynasty.
I buried it like your mother's voice.
I live in new elegance.

Oh come now, forces of night,
rename the daylight.
Show me salvageable.
Unleash the historical anti-drama.
Post up a fresh and sour taboo.
I see the sun, hanging hard in blinding dazzle.
Show me how to do that.
Show me how to be a giraffe
floating its head above the tree line of misery,
closer to something illuminated
in the night.

# IF YOU BUY AN OLD POLYGRAPH AT A SWAP MEET, DO NOT BREAK IT OUT AT A PARTY

When I first brought the thing home
I had no idea it would change me for the better.
I am an honest man
and that has made me a monster.

Now, I cannot trust lovers or anyone with curly hair.
The clerk at the supermarket wants my life.
The hairdresser keeps looking at my neck
and then the scissors
and then my neck.
I don't trust you. Your pants are baggy.
You've got choking hands.
All dresses are fingerprint recording devices.
I don't trust your painted face.
I don't like that you keep looking down or that your eyes
shift into neutral...
like a dying man's...
as a dying man's.

How do you know what is honest anymore?
Because your snotty toddler is not the most adorable thing in the world?
Acknowledge the sea otter.
The cops don't actually want you to have a nice day
after they slide you a ticket.
Cops are paid liars, breaking the law to keep the law,
speeding after speeders.
You are not the world's best grandma and didn't even apply in time?

Because that chocolate is not to die for unless you were a dog
and then you'd just be a dead dog?
Baby food, onion powder, caffeine, grapes, mushrooms, beer,
all the stuff I love is Hooch poison.
They don't tell us that cause it might harm sales for dog owners.
Many divorced people are still alive and death did not do them part.

I trust the machine.
You can trust something without a heartbeat, but it's nothing.

At the party, everyone practiced cheating the machine
through breathing techniques,
biting of the tongue,
thumbtacks in elbow skin
and various squeezing of butt muscles.

It didn't matter.

"Have you ever wanted someone more than me?"
"Have you ever lied to me?"

The slightest pause in their spouse's answer means gather the jackets.
Everything honest ends in silence.

# Frozen Valuables Catalogue

Walking fast through the Bowery.
Someone was selling 9/11 memorabilia.

It was all made in Taiwan.

One photograph of a child covered in dust,
holding our flag and a picture of someone.
One photograph of a set of mini-blinds,
tweaked up in a tree.

I felt white anvil.

Can you imagine someone selling a postcard of your mini-blinds?

I watch TV when I feel alone.

One night there was a piece on
about a collection of watches
at the Oklahoma City bombing memorial.
All stopped at the same time.
Some crushed. Some perfect. On display at the museum.

What are they worth?

The evening came on
out the window like glitter
in a widow's bonnet.

# The Project Known As X-ray

My real name is Lytle S. Adams. It is 1944 and I am feeling every bit of 52 years old. They call me Six Three. I'm tall. As friendly as anyone in my neighborhood. By trade, I am a dentist, a good one. I sometimes miss my patients while working this new project and I ring them to make sure they aren't taking in too much peanut brittle.

I have to tell you something that I haven't been able to shake.

I had a dream over a year ago and it woke me in the middle of the night.

There were bats. There were millions of bats scattered in the air above me and they seemed like they were waiting for me to speak. I am not sure how I knew this. I watched them and I was not afraid. When I spoke, they formed a tornado around me. The words I spoke to the bats were,

"Die for me."

Screeches. I hear it when cars peel out.

In the morning, I drew plans for a new bomb. A bat bomb. I did not get my hopes wrapped up too deeply in this project and I didn't want folks to gain interest on account of it being a far-fetched idea, so I kept the idea to myself and only a few close friends.

Ya see, when you send a letter to Washington, you don't expect anyone to read it. The White House, at this point in the war, was as desperate as every American to end the damn thing. I mailed them my idea, knowing they wouldn't read it, but they did. They were hearing every idea in the book. I was told, President Roosevelt himself was responsible for giving the go on the funding. They approved a somewhat limitless amount of funding for a three-year development time frame for my idea and called it Project X-ray.

I told them that I thought it was entirely possible to hem the loss of life on the battlefield using a type of bird to bring incendiary devices into the attics of homes among the city of the enemy. These would be timed explosions that would indeed kill these poor animals and burn lots of property, but for the sake of saving our God-fearing soldiers on the ground. It seemed worth it to all of us.

In my approximation, one sortie could drop two thousand of these types of bombs that would spread into countless fires. They would be slow burns so that the civilians could evacuate, but they would cause a paper type of structure to spread the fire quickly among the rest of the buildings in any Japanese city.

I recommended we use bats due to their strength. First, we could find millions of them in a few locations, dormant in Austin, Texas. Second, bats, especially females, are strong enough to carry more than their own weight. This is key for the timed incendiary device. Third, bats hibernate, and while sleeping they do not require food or complicated upkeep to stay alive. Fourth, bats fly in darkness and find secretive places (often in buildings) to hide when the sun is out. We set the timers to go off at dawn when the bats scramble into the eaves and attics to hide from sunlight. They are a natural covert force that moves swiftly through the evening. Little weird looking heroes if we can get it right.

Rex, my friend in advertising said, "Can you imagine hearing bombs fall through the sky and the sudden relief of quiet as there is nothing exploding, no noise at all, only to see a few thousand soaring bats coming through the moonlight like a plague? It would scare the bejeezus out of me. And the fires in the morning, like everyone had gone mad and decided to burn down their own home. It's like a passage out of Revelation. How did you come up with this stuff?"

I said, "It could be scotch? I'd like to think it came from a good place, even though it sounds a tad bit horrific. All I can think of right now is that X can do some good. Less Japs will die. Less of our boys die. It's butchery out there."

I spent six months devising a way to make bomb-shaped casings with little compartments, each containing a Mexican Free-tailed Bat from the caves and bridges of southern Texas. Each bat had a fountain pen-sized, timed, incendiary bomb strapped to it, right under their small bellies, the way they hold their young in flight. Dropped from five thousand feet from a bomber, the casings would deploy a parachute in mid-flight and then they would open to release the bats. They would then go roost in the nooks of the city and then burn.

After months of testing in Carlsbad, the Pentagon informed me that the target for Project X-ray was the industrial town of Osaka Bay. We were making great progress and had now devised a way to release 1,040,000 bat bombs in one sortie from just a few bombers. It was time to move to Dugway in Utah where the Army had built a fake Japanese city. We were going to try and set it all ablaze.

It was something. The National Defense Research Committee observer stated: "It was concluded that X-ray is an effective weapon." The chief of incendiary testing at Dugway wrote to us: "A reasonable number of destructive fires can be started in spite of the extremely small size of the units. The main advantage of the units would seem to be their placement within the enemy structures without the knowledge of the householder or fire watchers, thus allowing the fire to establish itself before being discovered."

The way that small fake city burned: so fast. It all became real. Thousands of fires moving like the angel of death through the paper and pine. I couldn't imagine people running through that maze. It smelled like hell. The smoke was turning the entire sky to hazel. In eight minutes, all that was left were the bones of buildings.

I spoke with one of the Brigadier Generals in confidence. I expressed my concern for having such a large part regarding the inception of such a destructive and strange weapon. He assured me that there would be time for the civilians to exit their homes since most of the home fires would be started in the attic and most of the Japanese slept near the floor, on the first floor. "It's better than obliterating an entire city like Dresden. Your idea is as humanitarian as war can get, my friend."

It was a small comfort. He was right. It was better than any alternative for destroying a city. That sentence sounds so strange. "A better way to destroy a city . . . ."

I was allowed to go to the bomber prep area and examine the canisters before one of the test drops. The room was very dark and smelled like a jetty full of seagulls. I was near one of the casings that wasn't finished being loaded and sealed. I could see the bats loaded in, like a revolver. Cozy. Unaware of the horror strapped to their chests. I touched the fuzz on one of their foreheads. It was soft. It was very soft. It did not open its eyes, but I could see its hand or paw. Little fingers like a baby. They were beautiful.

"See ya on the other side, Mack. Win this for us."

It was the summer of 1944 when everything took a turn for the absolute worst.

Our team received a letter from Fleet Admiral Ernest J. King telling us that our program had been suspended indefinitely. It was like a chimney fell from the sky onto our hands. Millions of dollars, thousands and thousands of dead bats and countless working hours, all out the door.

"Sir, can you explain this? Can we get some clarification on this?"

"We don't have clearance to tell you what the military is going to do, but we are shifting our focus to a different type of bomb. Project X-ray is estimated at taking another year to perfect. This alternative is ready to go."

"What is the alternative, General?"

"I am not at liberty to say."

"Is it more humanitarian than using the bats?"

"I can assure you, Six Three, that there will be no bats used for the military's other classified bomb project. I have been told it could end this whole thing. And yes, I'm sure it is far more humanitarian."

He smiled as he reached out his hand. "You have served your country well, Six Three."

"Mr. Adams. Lytle Adams. I'm a dentist."

"I never knew that. The United States Army could use a good dentist. I'll see you when this war is over. God bless you, Mr. Adams. You are a servant of the people, and on behalf of my fellow Americans, we thank you and are grateful."

He got in his Jeep and it was over. I thought, "Grateful for what?" I don't know what they did with the rest of the living bats.

I still have the dreams. I fall asleep and the tornado comes. The noise spins around me. I can't tell if those are bats swirling around me or children cloaked in black. They are waiting for me to speak. I choose not to.

# THE REGULAR

A regular, a drunkard, turns from the bar
staggering toward the staring group of college girls,
"I have my reasons," he says.
The girls just stared at each other
and their eyes were beautifully misled.
I knew that what he said
would be a great thing to say
before
blowing your brains out
on national television.

# Ramp Agent at 5:30 A.M.

My guys on the morning shift would have to meet them face to face. I ironed my jumpsuit for the first time in four years. Strange morning. The Marines were coming to speak to us "rampies." All the bag tugs parked, washed, beaten and ready.

The load control agent told us we would be briefed by the Marines.

Mike spoke with the Gunnery Sergeant directly. They spoke for about ten minutes and Mike came back to our station and we huddled around him.

"It's gonna be caskets."

Mike asked if we had any questions. We were quiet for about thirty-seconds and then the hands started to raise.

"Do we salute them?"

No.

"Will the Marines handle the load bearing shift?"

We don't touch the caskets until they are inside the aircraft, supervised by their detail.

"Does the warehouse agent take charge of the load sheet or does a Sergeant?"

I got it.

"Do the off-loaders place the caskets onto the push-tugs or the Marines?"

We drive the push-tugs. They will unload them from the deuce and a half trucks onto the tugs. They will off load the tugs onto the conveyor belts. Then we take over, inside the aircraft. Also, No jokes, No smiling. No sandbagging. All pro, all respect. I don't have to explain, check?

"Check."

Anything else?

"Are there other people on this flight."

Yes.

"So we arrange their luggage around the caskets? It ain't no secret that luggage gets stacked. We can't stack those caskets."

I am not sure how this is going to work until they get on the plane. I'll talk to the gate about limiting the passengers onboard. One more question, then let's get to work.

"If there are animal pens, do they go next to the caskets?"

Yes. Heated as normal.

Once in the aircraft, we shifted the caskets into position. A dog encased in plastic housing was terrified and loud. I have seen dogs freak out, but not like that. I can't imagine what the dog was thinking.

We slid our passenger bags around the coffins. Every move slow and deliberate. All along the dank cargo hold, new flags draped and pinned at the corners. Colored baggage among mostly black luggage.

One of the younger Marines was very helpful and was passing me bags. I asked,

"That casket by the wall looks loose. Should I slide this bag between the two caskets so it doesn't shift around during flight...so he doesn't shift...around during flight? I'm sorry. I've never...done this before."

He said, "I have and I still don't know what I'm doing. Don't beat yourself up. You can put the bag between the two coffins."

They said we should leave the hull of the plane so the detail could make its final check. I wondered what I would feel if these Marines that helped us load the plane went to lay down in those boxes. When the cargo door closed, we all saluted. I imagined it was all off to be buried in the sky.

# THE SABOTEUR

You say you're paying for drinks
after I already pass out in the talented shape of Robert Downey, Jr.

You want to ride bikes on Vietnamese sunshine
and I already sold mine for a motor full of wine
and creaking moonlight.

You want heavy metal suicide dinner
but I just started doing the dishes with lemon fresh Joy.

You gave me the day off only after I find out it is Slut Awareness Day
    at the factory.

You want a Christmas of electric sex
after I already smashed your long-legged lamps.

You want me to organize your gospelmatic China shop
and I just shot up the place with bull power!

You dressed up like a high voltage holiday
and I had to open your presents early.

You wanted a glacier vacation from hot poverty
so I screwed you with the freezer wide open.

Everything crushed can turn all citrus and gold!
Your fillings are gold. Mine, tangerine. Let's crush.
Let's lose. Let's loose. Lousy and loose. Blousy in juice.

# THE SECRET FOREST DYNASTY

We used a type of ripsaw
to cut the pipe cleanly for horseshoes.

That weekend the fireflies were out and touring.

They came at dusk as the pipe sparks
zipped into the air.

The fireflies, chasing them
and trying to catch the tiny moment of fire in their arms.

All of the fireflies
confused
that none of the sparks
wanted to run away with them,

to the place where fireflies
hide
and learn
to burn
all their lives
at the first signs
of darkness.

# The Healer

## CHAPTER 1

At some point in the vanishing history of a couple,
their home fades from a place of shelter to a museum
of what once was.

There are no new pictures.

The picture light above the painting of Avalon is busted;

the island is timeless in constant Pacific twilight.

A medical degree yellows in an Old English font.

The front door looks locked but doesn't lock.

The carpet smells like El Paso.

The cobweb motels on the ceiling corners have been vacated.

The trophies have become what all trophies become.

A typewriter is frozen and lost.

This couple hasn't reached age 40, but disease has made their home smell

convalescent and dank.

An ashtray is flooded with cremated nerves.

These nights are rubber and long.


## CHAPTER 2

Years ago, they picked up a widow's Steinway at an auction; it is the
only artifact in the house that has ever been dusted. The scent of
lemon wax and oil wafts from the oak of its hammered black gown.
The piano lid stays open, always, and a Polaroid of Margaret's face

rests there. The picture shows a wild softness in the mouth and something else in her cheekbones. It sits on the tray where the music is supposed to be read. He never thought music was something you should have to read.

Dr. Steve Timmerman is a fine pediatric doctor and a failed pianist. "My dad used to tell me at recitals, "every decent man fails at something that he wanted more than anything." He sits at the keys like a hunter in a deer outpost, waiting for melody to sneak by so he can pin it down under his fingers. As Margaret lay in the next room, coughing up colors, he kills the keys through the California evening. With every wrong note, he is reminded of how much he misses the smoke of her voice.

His interest in progressing as a musician deteriorated long ago when his obsession with obtaining a medical degree took hold. Since high school, he imagined that a successful career was connected to a successful love life. His parents were broke, miserable and slept in separate beds. His plan paid off when he met Margaret at Columbia University. She had a problem with burping out loud in the library. He offered to pat her back and weaseled his way into a first date by sliding his request in between the many technical benefits of a good burp. Since then, he has never wanted to leave her side.

Eight years of marriage saw its share of difficult times. It would be unfair not to mention that these times were often overpowered and blurred by an honest fascination and admiration for each other. They never knew love as a mad affair with sex on subways and the claw marks of jealousy. They had a steady love and slow evenings. A perfect night usually consisted of a pizza and some craft like when they made paper airplanes for Tobias, her nephew.

Margaret couldn't make a normal paper airplane. It was never a normal anything. Margaret's paper airplanes always had atomic banana missiles, turrets in non-aerodynamic places, secret refueling areas and at least one escape pod.

Steve loved Margaret's creativity and tried to chase it with logic.

"I think you should call it an escape hatch, honey. Boys know the difference between escape hatch and escape pod."

Margaret steels her focus on the X-Acto knife. "Thank you, NASA, but I know the difference and I am making the escape pod so it can go down the escape hatch."

"What's the tinfoil for?"

"That's a fire proof love letter launcher that won't burn up when it passes the sun or when satellite lasers try to take it out 'cause it looks like a foreign probe. It's very handy when the pod gets lost in orbit without communication. I dunno... just standard issue stuff."

She would get lost in a project and he would soon be lost in her, staring at her intense relationship with just a piece of paper, his crap plane with its popsicle stick refueling rod and sturdy wings still parked on the desk's tarmac.

He remembers how she cussed when she sliced her finger. He remembers fetching her a Band-Aid that night. In the morning, the bed was covered in blood.


CHAPTER 3

Steve had dove deep into the study and experimentations on cell research related to Von Willebrand disease. Margaret started experiencing the symptoms of the disorder about two years ago.

All the grant applications had been submitted.

They were ignored.

There are more people mating with horses than people carrying her disease.

Who cares?

Normally, not even him.

He poured over medical journals like a dumpster diver.

Margaret had become bedridden.

She was always cold.

He noticed blankets in department stores now.

His colleagues knew she had between one and six months to live.

No one could tell him to his face.

Steve tried to set up small fundraisers, but Margaret shot every concept down.

"Honey, I think your effort and your attention to me has been so sweet. But to be honest, I feel too guilty. Don't you remember watching those celebrities on television hosting those tear-jerking telethons for…I dunno…MS or cancer but probably wouldn't give a shit about it if they hadn't contracted it themselves so—"

Steve jumped in, "This isn't a congratulatory thing so we can pat ourselves on the back. So many people love you—the kids in your class, your family, everyone. I am only suggesting that we have the vision or…grace to accept their help. I could do so much more if I could just get some funding. If research persists, research prevails."

"I know the point you're trying to make and I know that your motives are out of…ya know…I know they're pure. But it's us, ya know? The world shouldn't care about Margaret Timmerman's poor blood clotting any more than they should care about your bad golf swing—too many problems out there."

The doctor stared at his terrible carpet full of coffee stains and blood. "My golf swing kicks ass and you know it."

They would often cut the drama of their conversations with a competition. Which of them could achieve the most sensational, the most bizarre, the most banal soap-opera sappiness?

"Oh, Johnny Thunderstick, you know I love you, even though you have the athletic skills of a twelve-year-old homosexual."

"I used to love you, Patches McGigglesquirts, until you poisoned my ferret in an unspeakable act of homophobic sexual defiance! I beseech you."

Margaret tossed her arms toward him. "I don't even know what beseeching is, but I think I beseech you, too, and I'll keep on beseeching you until the day I die. Now go in the kitchen and make me something. And not soup. Your soup sucks."

"It's canned."

"I know. You should write the company."


CHAPTER 4

He bathed her pudgy body. It was so badly bruised, she couldn't stand to have the shower water strike the back of her legs. He could only barely touch her skin due to the spreading of the sores. He missed sex only when he bathed her. He imagined the moans that emanated from the pain in her limbs to be the moans of something more erotic.

"I think you're beautiful."

She moved the soap slowly across her stomach. "Oh, sure with my white face and my hair falling out and the purple skin and black blotches. I wish I knew this was your taste back when I was shaving my legs and plucking my eyebrows. "

"Do you remember, Marge, when you told your class you were bruised 'cause you got jumped into the Crips, but left because their program was impacted?"

"I don't think they knew what 'impacted' means. I started telling them you'd beat me cause you didn't get enough croutons. Conditioner. Thanks."

"Margo, I really like your big nose and I like squeezing your hand. I like noticing the cracks and the little line things about it. When I squeeze it, I feel something good shoot through my body. It's weird. You do look better."

She leaned forward toward the faucet. Her face had flashed into somberness.

"I look better? I feel so much worse. Steve, I just want it to be over. I'm not kidding. The pain is ...this is so ..." Her tears dropped into the bath. Concentric circles spun towards the porcelain walls.

He leaned over the clouded bathwater as the bubbles crackled. "I was going to tell you that there are some new theories about the medicines you've been taking—

"I don't want any more medicine. I don't want people to send any more cards saying they're praying for me. I don't want anything. Prayer isn't working. Medicine isn't working."

Steve's brow crunched. "Just give me time. I can't tell you how shitty I feel about being a doctor and having all these connections and still not being able to do anything for you. I can't stop trying."

Margaret's wet and stringy hair tilted back. "I'm not supposed to be fighting this, honey. I don't know how you have this unrealistic hope. I don't think you would if you knew how I felt. What do I have, a week? Two weeks? I am tired and I think . . . I'm just done."

Steve released a shot of hot water between her legs.

"If you kill yourself, I'll sue you."

He kissed her forehead and whispered something else in her ear.

She stared into the murk.

Her hand moved through the soap bubbles like a razor through snow.


CHAPTER 5

It was 1:26 in the morning when Steve arrived at the UCI student research labs. It was here, on a steady diet of coffee and crumb donuts, where he had spent every free hour attempting various combinations of chemical reactions to create a medicine that would cause platelets to clot quickly for those with her condition. He decided against telling her in case his theories were wrong.

Only two Danish doctors had come close to a cure and Steve had sussed them for all their documents, lab evidence, and recent findings. Then, he made a discovery of his own. One of the rats infected with the disease had significant clotting after being treated with a crushed pill form that rushes blood and platelets to a wound or scar. The only problem was that the acceleration of the clotting was much quicker than a human's normal response to clotting. Doctor Timmerman needed a person to try his formula on.

Tomorrow, he would put an anonymous ad in the paper for volunteers and hope that money would come to pay them after the trial was over. Whether it was junkies, homeless people or students, it wouldn't matter to him. Time was running out.

Before he turned out the lights to the lab, Dr. Timmerman caught a glimpse of the stainless metal tray in front of him and the small pile of pills. He knew that he couldn't ethically give a possibly lethal dose of medicine under the auspices of a clinical trial. He could feel frustration curdle in his fingernails. He was stuck.

He quickly lifted a scalpel to his forearm and made a one-and-a-half inch incision. The blood globbed onto the cold Formica. He was exhausted from the countless hours of testing that it seemed to hurt less. It still smarted like a son-of-a-bitch, just a little less.

He placed half of the gray pill on his tongue and let it dissolve, felt it slip into his gums and under his tongue.

Five minutes later, his lungs reacted first. It felt like a good dose of oxygen was pushing its way out. Gripping the wound on his arm, he waited. He thought about Margaret in that tub hours earlier-- the one with the lion's paws at the bottom-- and how she always made a prune comment whenever she got out and he remembered how he loved that.

His senses were sparkling.

He noticed everything about his body:

The turning in his stomach from forgetting to eat.

The cold feeling between his socks and skin.

The wet, hot sear on his forearm.

The creaking in the bones of his shoulders.

A desperate gurgling down by his liver.

And then, exhaustion.

He fell asleep with his hands in front of him, as if playing a piano in the air.


CHAPTER 6

Two hours later, Steve awoke with drool cooling his cheek. The wound had almost completely healed. His eyes widened as if he were a kid watching miracles on TV. He thought to himself, "My God, I only took half a dose." He felt like a dart had lodged in his neck from passing out on the desk.

He thought, "What does this mean? What could this mean?" He went to call one of his colleagues, a friend from Dartmouth. As he reached for the phone, he noticed that three of his fingers, between pinky and thumb, were slightly sealed together, on each hand. "What the...?" As he forced his sealed fingers apart, blood emerged.

He looked around the table for glue that he might have dropped his hand across while sleeping, but there was none. The skin between each digit had grafted to itself.

As he drove to their home from the lab, Dr. Timmerman kept turning up the FM radio a couple more notches every few minutes. He wondered if he was losing signal and saw that the volume was now maxed out. It took forty minutes for him to realize that the holes of his ears were also slowly healing.


## CHAPTER 7

It was 6:45 in the morning, and the light on the highway was breaking across the lane's reflectors. He called his wife.

"Margaret." His voice thumped dull in his head as if in a thick plastic drum. "Something has happened. I might need you to help me. Oh, and I might need some of your nail polish remover and eardrops. I'll be home in, like, twenty. I can't talk now. I'll explain later. Sorry for waking you. I love you."

She might have said something, but it was hard for him to hear. He hoped she had answered the phone.


## CHAPTER 8

Steve could feel his heartbeat increase rapidly. The insides of his arms felt like Japanese rice. His lips became chapped in the corners and stretched. He stumbled up to the garage, removed his shoe and tore his sock from his skin. Bits of black cloth had fused with the flesh. His toes were becoming one lump and it threw his balance out of whack.

Wondering whom to call for help, he stumbled into the kitchen, but then realized he still wouldn't be able to hear if anyone was answering. His pores were stretching and this cold burning sensation caused him to cry like he was lost in a department store. He scratched a note with a marker in big block letters.

Steve sat down at the piano, while Margaret slept nude in the next room. With the knuckle of his right hand he pressed a D note, then a G, then an A. He waited. He felt the piano vibrate under the knobs of his hands, but he could only hear the shifting and growing pulse of skin inside his skull like diving into the deep end. The slow sobbing broke the skin on the sides of his mouth and his lips were now bleeding.

He saw himself in the black reflection of the piano lid and watched as the blood in the corners of his mouth quickly morphed into flesh.

Red, then pink, then white, then pink, then beige.

His eyelids ached like they were made of nickel.

Steve gently pried one eyelid open with the side of his thumb.

He could see the photo of Margaret, frozen on the piano, resting there like one page of a great, short symphony. He stared at it and knew it would be the last time. His thoughts poured out like notes: "You were mine. You were my life and beautiful and unlucky. You were music. You were my music."

He went to the cupboard and struggled to crush up two dozen sleeping pills. He placed them in a glass of water and then stepped into the room where she slept. Steve placed the glass and the note on her nightstand beside her unfinished crossword puzzles. He fought to breathe through a narrow passage in his nostril, pushing out air like a thoroughbred.

He saw the shadow of her lips in the gray light. He gently pressed his mouth to her neck. He wanted to kiss her, but could only bump against her tender skin. His mouth was now fully sealed.

Screams of agony were muted in his chest as he removed his clothes.

He lifted the sheets that smelled of her favorite fabric softener. She lay there on her side, heavy in sleep. He pressed his body to hers, then gently grasped her hand for the last time. He felt warm and terrified.

He tried to relax. In the morning she would find the note and the glass. The note had just two sentences. "I will see you soon." That was the first. The second sentence, written frenetic and fumbling, seemed to hold an entire species' misery in the tiniest bit of space: "I tried."

As he pressed closer to her, the skin above his eyes began to seal over.

He moved the sticky bubble gums of his hands to the thigh of his woman.

He was glad they were alone there, in that room.

The curtains held back the sunrise.

The alarm clock remained silent.

Unsalvageable bodies.

He knew that, soon, they would be one.

Days later, a coroner will approach.

Removing his mask outside the rancid home,

he will remove a cigarette and imagine the conversation

a mortician will have with their families,

gently and tastefully suggesting one tombstone,

one grave,

and one casket.

# CHURCH OF THE BROKEN AXE HANDLE
*(for B. W.)*

Lord, my friend's heart has disassembled.
So broken, it is red dust.
His pen is rust.
His body is not a house built for silent prayer.
It is a church of blood, raw and razor pumping
for that scar power, axe handle snap and dirt face gospel.

We belong to the same church.

Our clergy: blacksmiths and cut throats,
former party murderers
and never again to be bound choir.

Our lobby holds a bowl of holy water
filled with terrified jellyfish.
Come wash your hands in it again.
Feel the frenzied sting of his creatures.
It is the Lord's idea to have the sting.

Every bee zap, every lion's tooth, every elephant stomp,
every ounce of venom is born from the Lord's creative grasp,
violence he sees in his Milky Way ghost wild head.

The fear of the poisonous bite.
The jaws rumbling and clacking hungry.
The noise groaning and gaining on you in the woods.
The bite.
The relief of the antidote.
The sweet shock of the safe cold river.

We choose to call all these things, The Lord.

Not the Slaughter Lord,
not the Unbolted Hateful Lord,
not the Lord at War,
not the Author of Gnashing Hell and the Angel Ranks,

No, we call upon our Lord,
the phantom flesh Lord that loves you and made you to get up again.
Our Lord is the Lord of the moray eel incisors.
The Lord of the whale carcass and glossy shark speed.
The Lord of the vampire bat swamp bones
and crocodile gut stomp.
The Lord of the sleeping jaguar
and the Possum army moving their evil eyes through the twilight.
The tearing, the tearing. The nourishment.
We are the horror in the Lord's love poem.

This Lord is the Lord over us.
We do not call on him as some statue with a trimmed beard,
man-sandals and archaic language that never knew science.
He has given birth to us to sing in the fight.
We are the organ full of bees, enemies of silence.
Sing out your death rattle constant.
Sing out your questions with the force and mess of dynamite stew.
Listen for an answer echoing,
spinning warmth inside you like a Leslie speaker.

You will hear it when you are so alone
you wish someone would come and try to kill you
just to hear what your cries to heaven sounded like
when heaven was listening.

I know you are alone and soaking in it
like solitude is blood
and the night is the letting.

Your heart races
with the pressure
of everyone in the room
finding a slow dance partner
but you.

Tap in. Tap the shoulder.
Love is yours.
Make the first move.
Lose the ones who stepped on your shoes.

Love is yours.
Let it be its horrible self. Learn it.

Our church is fully armed. Return to it with devotion.

Your spirit is a ready gun. Load it yourself.
Only fire it into the worthy.

Rise above the grief bait and sugars of sorrow.
Spin searing gold from all that copper noise.
You are better than the demons whispering in your cheeks.

The floors of self-doubt are weak.
Do not fall where the heavy have fallen.

Lift us into your belief, let it blast.
Let it be a bloodbath
with your innards on the floor,
no apologies.

Welcome yourself to ugly glory, you.

This is not typical church.
We will not yell
about sin and hell
for that picture doesn't work anymore
for those who have worked on its factory floors.

We welcome you, you new crawling psalms,
you drunk choirs
you gouged melodies
you nasty bags of glowing mercy.
We welcome those with unpaid bone tariffs
those raised by the missing
those boys who got lost in the eyes of another boy
those who loved the cities that hated them
those who keep putting on their gloves for boxing the sanity out
those who couldn't scratch their golden tickets
because their nails were ground down
from clawing their own way out of their father's casket
those who couldn't get skinny enough to get to the front of the line

those who couldn't stand anymore
so they built splints out of words, out of their own words.
Depth charges, yes!
The choir charging the audience with tambourines in their teeth, yes!
Kick me when I'm up, yes!
Hallelujah, we are fucked! Yes!
Bring it on so we can lift ourselves out of the magpie swamp.
The worst thing you have ever been through is always a fair fight.

Come to the church of the new.
A building that only says lost and in bold letters, found.

This is not typical church.
This is a low attended funeral,
a skinny sinner bugger kegger,
a pietà full of doves that demands
beautiful release…

Buddy, you are church.
A house of healing that…
is the closest thing to the image of salvation
since people thought to hold hands
when jumping to their deaths from the failure of buildings.

Open the gates, my friend. Send St. Peter home.
All are welcome.
Turn on the golden lights.
Guide us in.
Someone you have been waiting for is coming.
Guard your heart minimally. Security threat, beige.
You can carry a knife and still trust everyone.

Carry it in your mouth.

Every time you open it,
we await the sharpening noise of worship.

Cry out into the darkness
the sermon that doesn't cease:
You cannot be abandoned.
You can only be released.

# THE RETURN OF CHRIST

Trying to let go of you
is like trying to spit out my teeth
before the dashboard
roars into my throat.

Something lonely in the air has over-ripened the fruit.

I want her to return to me tonight, to my ship,
but I don't wanna do anything different in my life.
I don't want to be a fresh lure.

I want her to be warm, here, arms full of cake,
still shaped like a broken white viola.

Some piano is being beaten to death outside.
That's my kind of music.
That's the night music the kids are all choking on.
I close the hatches of my boat.

It's so still in here, I can't write anything
but the songs of divers,
falling into something very quiet.
The more I sit here and eat this poem,
the more my clothes don't fit.
The more my spaghetti brains and stubborn bruises show.
I need a drink.

All booze is just a sleeping pill now.
I close my eyes. Love.
You taste like someone waving.

Sometimes living is a Swiss Bliss
and sometimes it's a rotten popsicle.
The difference between bad living and bad loving
is a slipped keystroke.
The return key is big and easy,
not as easy as the space key.

I can imagine people here with me.
They speak in the creaking of aluminum masts.
Comes and goes in waves.

I tell them I do want her to return. They ask:
Do I have the gear to make that happen?

If Christians can wait this long for their savior to return
on an unknown open-ended invite of prose,
I can wait a few years for my beautiful wand
to soar from some black ship, no longer adorning the bow
in gold paint and oak,
penetrating the coastal showgirls with her harbor light.

The night turns to straight coffee.
Channel 16 is for distress signals only
and I listen all night.
I wonder if I will hear the voices again
while staring at something shiny
sinking in the water.

# The Honest Savior

*I have been trying to reach you.*

My arms are tingling.

*Yes. This is the Lord and you said you wanted to talk. Here I am. You are not inventing this dialogue. It is true; you are asleep. I am here with you. I have always been with you.*

Always? Forgive me but…even during lovin'?

*When your heart was in it, yes. Sometimes I couldn't stand the hollow thumping sound and I left your body. I know you heard me leaving.*

That explains much. I have some questions I have been meaning to ask you, Lord.

*Good. This is why I have come. I have some questions I have been trying to ask you.*

Question 1: Is it working? Is this great experiment working?

*Not exactly the way I envisioned it. I decided to let it unfold. Other universes where I controlled too much, there was much less beauty. Much less horror, but much less beauty.*

So why not just wipe us out and start over?

*I am not as cruel as your Bible makes me out to be. Also, it seems you might not need my help.*

You said my Bible, is it not your Bible that you wrote or breathed into every word?

*If I am the author of consciousness and breath, then in a way, every word is God-breathed. The problem I have with the Bible is that each individual's experiences shape interpretation. If you look at the harshness in the Old Testament and the miracles of blood and the jealousy, the angels of death, the commands to attempt to kill your son, the sacrifices of animals, the stoning of sinners, the thirst for choosing sides in war, turning a woman to salt for looking*

*at something...compared to me when I came during the New Testament...*
*it doesn't match. The kings did remove many books; they should've removed*
*more and put in what I was telling them.*

I expected you to speak in Old English or Greek for some reason.

*I know no language and I know all languages.*

What? That's confusing.

*I know, I'm joking. Many humans expect me to communicate in riddles*
*and mystic visions. Some thouest think I am locked into old timey language.*
*Humans were dumb when the Bible was written. I am not back then, I am*
*now and I am only then when reticent. I can speak through music or any*
*language. It is all just noise, sometimes it is a wonderful noise.*

What about the whale or the mighty fish that Jonah got eaten by and
miraculously did not drown or get digested by?

*Show me a fish that would want to swallow a man. Show me a man that*
*would not kill himself after such a gross experience. If I invented the rules of*
*physics, I do not need to break them to make myself known. I don't hurt people*
*to make a point. Be good. Be fair. Care for the poor. Know my name. Respect*
*me. Thank me. Speak to me. Don't treat me like human royalty. Royalty is*
*a strange invention of the people.*

What do you think of worship music?

*Ahhhhh...I love the sweet sound of song. Music is a language I thrive upon*
*and make every creature immediately understand, even if it is not appreciated.*
*That being said, I do not really like worship music. I love David's poetry and*
*it was coming from a place of purity and not tradition. He broke into song.*
*That is a feeling that is true. If people broke into song, I'd feel it. I am not*
*so shallow that I need humans to tell me how amazing I am, as the insecure*
*kings of the past did. Appreciation is one thing, but worship is not necessary for*
*me to show love or to receive it.*

I want to talk about Lucifer. Is there mercy for angels? Tell me about
Hell.

*Hell is dying and feeling like you didn't love and live completely. It is laying in your regrets, forever. Mercy is earned. Lucifer is gone. He has no power. What was in him is in you. Some can squash it.*

Is the Bible perfect?

*No. Nothing touched by man is perfect.*

Did you change from the jealous God to the God who loves all?

*It is safe to say that I do not change. That deity that the storytellers feared was not me. I do not thrive off fear. I am compassion where there is no room for compassion. I am hope in things unseen. I am rain in the desert. Boastfulness has driven men away from me, as well as bad stewards, the haughty, greedy so-called messengers of my character.*

*Every church with a pastor in a luxury car makes me want to puke.*

What about drinking?

*I drank when I was on earth. I liked it very much. Someone should've documented how often. Plenty. It was safer than most water. It is no secret that too much of anything can lead to folly. Too much marshmallows even can wreck you. Trust me. I am so saddened by all these rules that are in the good intention of getting closer to my character, but an absolute waste of time.*

Speaking of your character, did the temple scene happen where you, as Jesus, got angry and flipped the tables of the greedy gamblers and merchants?

*I did. Greed and hoarding, living too lush while your brethren starve angers me to no end. I do get angry, but I took it out on the tables, not the people.*

Where do you live? In churches?

*I don't hang out in churches. Do not misinterpret me. I love the church, but it was always meant as a place to gather and share ideas. It has become spectacle. Some churches clearly need their own temple table flipping scene and less fog machine.*

I agree. Here is one that boggles me. There is so much poetry and talking snakes and rules about stoning women and eating shrimp or pork in this Bible. Why not put out another Bible? Why not drop a clear manual for following your spirit?

*Because I can't trust humans to not make it into something for their own gains in power, war, and politics. Everything is twisted in the hands of men. I will speak to their hearts directly.*

And the last question: Heaven? Are there golden streets, pearly gates, and mansions?

*Not literally. My angels work hard but I am not going to send them to Earth to pillage a billion oysters to build a gate. And why would I need a gate? I have built a place that is light-years beyond gold and pearls. How peaceful can any community be with a large, expensive gate? I am a wondrous God but I will never be an illogical God. I am your God. Clear your heart and I will make myself at home.*

*There are no floating mansions. You know I can come up with something better than that.*

Have you ever met an atheist.

*Sure, but I know they might come around. People can feel it in their soul. Don't pester anybody, though. Remember the whole thief in the night concept? I was only trying to say…that's my style.*

# Please Welcome, Dick Richards, the World's Worst Poet

Hello, every *buddy*. As in friend. My name is Dick Richards.
The name is redundant
but the love is abundant x 2
Here is a poem I wrote for lovers. It is called
Even the Pope hates condoms.

I said to number 14,
Hey, Ma'am, you look like a porno shop.
She said, you mean 'cause I'm raw and sexy?
And I said no
'cause I could tell I'd be embarrassed to be inside you.

It works on paper. Ink.
When life hands you grapes,
eat a raisin…and if that raisin cartoon can sing like Marvin Gaye,
it will taste murdered.

May I pour classic wine down your vagina
and catch it in a bottle so I can sell it for less?

Let's have a Yankee Candle séance.
Let's dye our hair and watch The Craft.
I cast a spelling bee on you.

You will break off my stinger.

When I think of you naked, why do I think of scallops?

If the shoe fits, try to remember that
that is your size.

Not into me, lover?
Better to have lived and learned
than to have put this in your mouth.

If Kenny Rogers taught you origami,
would you know when to fold 'em?

# Van Morrison News Alert

I'm so out of the know,
I just found out that the song "Brown-Eyed Girl"
was about anal.

The waterfall part,
all that slippin' and slidin',
that whole "behind" the stadium bit
really sealed the deal.

# My New Tombstone

I can see you.

# When Your Friends Leave You

It always feels so great to feel you
hug me like a coked-up conga player.

You are one of the guys I know.

That sentence used to say "greatest guys I know"
but it is much funnier and true to say
you are definitely one of the guys I know.

I don't know if we drifted somewhere,
like crawdads in a rising riverbed,
but I know that when we do get around to being men,
we can hardly stomach
the plate full of nails
of saying I love you.

We always add some word to make it more palatable.

I love you, you prick.

We end up muttering it because either one of us almost died
or is moving further away than either of us can afford in airfare.

Don't go.

Who will walk into a bar with fake blood on his face
and order a beer like nothing happened?
Who will laugh when I pull a fake dove from my zipper
throw it on the dinner table before I exit, yelling, "Peace"?

So many of our brothers, raised by single mothers.
The quality broke sissies we were.
You were my blood and asphalt brother.
I remember being young and thinking of our current families
all cracked and desperate
like sycamores outgrowing the sidewalk.

I remember being confused and wondering why marriage
was so hard
and divorce, so convenient.
The city was tearing out all the strawberry fields
to put in warehouses. Everything good was going away.

As a kid I thought:
Can't people just talk,
screw, go on vacation so they can miss home,
and order a large pizza?

Thank God you and your woman found each other.
I see joy in your stride.
May your journey fill your heart with wild music
and may the music of Journey
fill your mind with don't stoppable believin'.

Errol Flynn is jealous and dead.

May you spread your gooey dorkiness
into the stiff mouth of the world.

See your friends in the faces and wonky nuances of others.
See the beauty in being missed
because some people are not.

I will always see you, running in the buff down the beach
at night into the glowing red tides of the sea, the green light
exploding around you like a force field.
I will see you drinking me out of my relational misery
into the better misery of the hangover.
I will still see you
dancing out the alcohol, spazzy on your good foot.
I will see you falling on a hill of powder and posing
with your face in your hands for the broken camera.
I will see the kid from the dumps of Bradford Place,
the buddy who was broke and unbreakable,
I love you, you asshole.

It is strawberry season.
What we came from is in the air and I miss you
like a son of a bitch.

# K2

A storm beyond the summit,
a blizzard of confetti
shreds your skin.

You don't conquer a mountain
by climbing it.

You only get to the top
to show yourself
how small and winded you are.
You can't conquer a mountain.
You just annoy it.

# SHELBY BOTTOMS

I had to get out of the house
because it was crunching me
and everything in it was dressed like her.

I was trying like hell to blank the day.
I had a nightmare which scared me enough
to sleep with a golf club.

I rode my bike to a park called the Shelby Green Bottoms.
It's a hilarious name because I imagine it is made up.

I came to a hill leading into the park and it was so fast my black
airborne cap flew off. The speed of the hill had made me do a little
dumb girl smile that I tried to fight back but couldn't. This whole
smiling thing is filling me with something. They are questions:

Did I take off my jacket near a sign that said: "Sixty European
Starling birds were released in New York's Central Park in 1890 to
commemorate one of the birds found in Shakespeare's work and now
there are two hundred million in the U.S. They must be captured
because they are killing off the native species . . ."?

Yes.

Did I see an eagle—a gazing eagle perched in the high tree line?

Yes.

Did I think of the Muppet, Sam the Eagle, and do the eagle's voice
for ten minutes?

Yes.

Did I see a strange single turret castle that had risen from the
Cumberland River?

Yes.

Was it actually for a water plant built in the 1940's?

No, I stand by it being a magic castle where sea monsters recharge and shine their weapons.

Did the massive General Jackson Riverboat come towards me with a bluegrass band playing Ring of Fire as hard as they could on their banjos?

Yes.

Did it make me feel like Disneyland was being born inside me?

Yes.

Did I find a file folder that said "Tim's Outreach Work" and there was nothing in it?

Yes.

Did it make me think of how empty I was feeling earlier?

Yes.

Did I see a batch of flowers at the end of a private airport landing strip?

Yes.

Did I try and pull some poetry from it and give up and just watch the planes land?

Yes.

Did the mailman wave at me when I entered the residential area on my bike?

Yes.

Did a fat white man say, "Howdy, how ya doin'?" when I rolled past his garden?

Yes.

I told him, "I'm fine. I'm doing fine. Thank you."

Did I mean it?

Damn right I did.

Some days are fat and happy
and they call you over to remind you
that doing nothing isn't.

# NASHVILLE, A LIST OF BULLET HOLES

How many people come here and have their future
slip through their fingers
though it had nothing to do with music?
Talk about God at the Gold Rush and forget what you said.
Tell someone strange goodnight and wake up next to them.
Kris Kristofferson lives in a waffle.
Romantic words I slung
as meaningless as a Christmas tree that doesn't die.
No poetry. My time here was a painting. Here are the colors:

Mercy lounge roller shoes.
The basement show and Merlin showing up.
The pool hall underground.
Loveless Café biscuits.
The Natchez Trace turkeys roaming past my Harley.
Spring Hill Applebee's dates.
My birthday at The Old School Café.
The coconut cake at the gas station.
Danbury Circle's overuse of Christmas decorations
and our rad neighbors who laughed.
Fixing furniture and calling my shop Brown's Den of Desire or something.
Fixing up local honey into a teal delight.
Poetry show in the yard as the night got warm and easy.
Party at the groove, my going away party, topless magic.
Five Points Wine and Marche sausage.
Taking Dad to the honkey tonks
and him feeling alive around a beautiful woman.
The lights going out at Alley Cat in the rain and them
staying open to give us free drinks.
The Red Door Saloon skeleton.
        Franklin Irish Pub and seeing the rays come off Ashley Judd.
Getting recognized at the Mellow Mushroom as the poetry dude.
Performing with Anis Mojgani in the arcade.
Racing the Cumberland showboat by bike alone, down in Shelby Bottoms.
Amanda in the snow.

Brandon and Josh launching
with the snowboard in Thompson Station Park for our one day of
   wonderland.
Thompson Station Grill, view of the cows and train, my dream house
   that never was.
Travis doing the commercial for Cape Cod Potato Chips
and doing a sweet running man.
Paint ball with David and poor Phil getting shot in the nuts.
Jeannie and Mark, sweet and wonderful, away at Marcy's funeral.
Recording with the kick-assedness of the Brownings!
The creek behind the house-for-fort building
and the green label Jack Daniels.
Rebecca and the gorgeous piano photos.
Ben and Jonathon dancing in their underwear for the spider party.
T.J. Graham radio show magic with David Cross
and Ben laughing hyena style.
Todd, Jamie, Rababa and Bingham rolling around for the BB gun summer.
PBRchery: archery into PBR cans.
Beer pong kitchen destruction.
White trash dice party and roman candle wars.
Poker nights in Spring Hill when the pizza guy invited himself to
   join in and wouldn't leave.
Disc golf at the park and laying down for the thunder.
Canoeing down the Duck River with only four beers to ration, tipping.
Lilly singing her lesbian magic.
Everyone dancing on Jonathon's car in the middle of the night
and crushing it to death.
Almost fist fighting at a fashion show when a douche tried to fight me
and my girlfriend getting bummed and I wanted her to say, screw that guy.
Cold War Kids show at Mercy with me on a drum, screaming words
   that wanted out.
Mogwai at Mercy Lounge
and everyone cheering when the guitars were raised. like guide-ons.
Sigur Ros at the Ryman in the pews with Erin Younger
and Jason go forth, AKA the Poopmaster.
Dan on his scooter, bearded and fully Christian.
All those drunk Christians.
Michael Mcdonald asking me to his party in Liepers Fork,
only to tell him Yeahmo Be There.

That condo that I thought would free us from junk but killed my love.
The Gary Auction and the bottles of Coke.
Sneaking booze into the amateur wrestling matches
in Columbia and Nashville.
The Belcourt to drink Jack and hear Mark Kozelek with Carver.
Debbie! The photo. Murdered!
Horseshoes with Josh Brown.
Hanging with Keckley in the cigar shop in Murfreesboro,
waiting for the Kings of Leon to blow each other up.
 Dancing at Phil and Kelly's barn in Columbia
and yelling colors at the trains passing.
St. Mark's church break-in with Johnny and seeing the poem unfold.
Motorcycling down West Harpeth Rd. with her holding me good,
until we stopped to watch The Wizard of Oz in the park.
The Tin Man song,
the Tin Man.
He is oiled.
This spaghetti western in the nightscape.
The bars on Broadway are radios
sweating when you sing like a controlled burn.

This Southern sky, our formal ballroom
for whiskey slipping in the daylight.
A town where it is okay to say
if you come at me, come at me with spirit,
all cluster-whipped and ready to start over.

If everyone's leaving for somewhere
where am I going?
I got this boat in the west waiting for me
and I will sleep in the arms of gentle rocking.
I will cruise out alone into the Island waters
and see our nation from afar
and wonder where you all are
and wish you could hear me say
I love you in firefly season.

I wish you
an uncomplicated bliss.

# CROSS COUNTRY MOTORCYCLE FRENZY

The Tennessee road curls like a jet black dragon.
A big fat bug explodes against your hand at 75 mph in Tulsa.
The wind in Amarillo wraps around your leather like old sandpaper.
The sunset is a red snapper that got away.
Your exhaust rumbles by your legs
and your friends are next to you
driving your car into the lights over California.
Welcome back to living your ass off.
Home is what you think of first
when you are in a hundred motels
trying to get some kind of life kick-started.

# GROCERY LIST

Be more forgiving.
Substitute "goodbye" for "I like your face."
Spend two nights a week not drinking to forget.
Listen to your body.
Listen to someone else's body.
Get limber.
Don't dog yourself to feel humble. It never works.
Lift others up onto your back until you are sore.
Write for yourself a movie that doesn't end.
Eat a churro slowly.
Kiss your mother on the cheek and don't miss.
Remember that now is barely now. It will soon be back then. Stop.
Don't text anyone while talking with anyone.
Finish everything.
Get Milk.

# GLOWING IN DENVER
*(for A.M.)*

At the evening's outdoor concert
among the Red Rock boulders
and thousands of Sigur Ros fans...
I noticed something peculiar—
no one was buying anything from the roaming vendors
who were selling glowing rabbit ears or
the rainbow necklaces, neon and burning,
or a blaze of dollar sign colors
that sparkled in the tight Colorado air.

That was stuff you sold at a dwindling rave reunion
or a Nelson concert
or a Phish (barf barf) jamfest.

No one in their right mind was going to buy one of these
expensive gags at a Sigur Ros concert, where strings and distortion
lull you into a breathless acid test.

No one except for good old tasteless me.
Fifteen dollars for a necklace that glowed with a money sign on it.
Lights attract me like I was a suicidal deer or a test tube soldier.
It was a treasure from the sunken lands of *Tron*
and I needed it.

Tonight,
I bought it for you, Anis.

I know you thought,
Crap. Now I gotta wear this damn thing.
I'm the only one.
It's pitch black
and I am glowing like a toxic idiot from Buckeye.

I went to the restroom and
as I walked toward my seat during the show
I could see you were covering
the battery powered nuisance some

with your jacket
but I was amazed you had it on at all.
It was poking out of the vase of your Iranian throat
that has never seen a decent necktie.
You looked like E.T. on tranquilizers
and you were signaling for home.

The concert was almost over…
You were still the only one.
What a triumph!
I bought it for you.
Can I tell you why?

To see you there,
a floral aurora in a sky of cell phone lights
reflecting on the black sea
of the hypnotized.

There you were,
bright and strange among thousands of folks
whose power had almost ran out.

One wild light, boiling in the stew of waiting believers.
This is how I see you.

That one light when all the other lights have gone out.
Bright Casanova of volume and soft shoe vaudeville.
Electric slide of "I am waiting for my one."
Atomic adorable creole and figgy passion.
You are the tracer bullet that aims us in the night.
A 1000-watt amp that awakes in the morning at 120 mph
to make chocolate shotguns for your battles toward love.
You are a man rowing upon the water at five a.m.
letting his spirit slide upon the glass,
refreshed and ready to give
when he returns, older, solitary and wild.

We are waiting for our batteries to be jumped.
We are the dark mass of open mouthed caverns.
Throw some meteors of your brawling light in—

Throw that southern gunpowder down our lungs.
Cough a spark.
Your chest is still glowing.
We are ready to burn.

We are pinned like medals to your greatness.

# Top

A soldier once told me,
*"Killing kills your sense of seeing the living as sacred.*
*Once you get that out of the way, you're not afraid to die out here alone."*

Master Sergeant JC and I write back and forth.
We went to the same basic training, Airborne school,
and were stationed in the same Airborne battery.
I got out from the 82nd and he stayed in to run the whole battalion,
fifteen years later. A huge, buff man with a laugh like a side of beef.
He is now guarding Highway 8 in Baghdad.
He has been advancing rapidly in the ranks.
I used to call him Sarge,
then Smoke,
now Top.

He told me about a meeting with his younger Sergeants
after the troops had been walking through Kut
and getting pot shots at them.
The Sergeants told him it was slaughter
to go in there without armored personnel carriers.

He relayed this info to get gear before the patrols
and the Captain relayed his orders back:
Patrols in Kut must continue on foot according to Centcom.

I started to ramble about the frustrations of military inefficiency.
There is a difference between talking to someone about war
and talking to someone in war about it.

"Don't do it, Derrick."
Do what?
"Don't make me feel like we're dying for nothing."
I won't. You aren't. They aren't.
"We are freeing these people."
Right.
"If we didn't do it, no one would've"
I know...

"I miss my wife, Derrick."
I talked to her. Cindy is good. The dogs are good.
"I miss Sam Adams beer a lot."
Can't help ya there. I could do a fine job describing the taste.
"We are getting picked off. We are wondering when can we fire at will
and have the soft targets off the list
and engage the enemy in
Mosques, all that."
Soon.
Wanna talk about beer?

Where am I, John?
Former Cannoneer #2, round loader, breech puller,
foxhole digger, non-rigger, fuse counter,
aiming pole runner, M60-toting,
ambush crushing grenadier, Specialist Brown is now
just a writer and I am proud of you.
I want you to remember home.

The bars here are full of laughter.
The ribs are falling off the bone.
Even Summer is coming home.
You can golf in the twilight.
I want you to miss these things.
I don't care who wins.
I want you to stay alive.
Keep your weapon clean.
Stay alert.
Stay alive.
Kill everything.
Fight everything.
Just stay alive, John.
Keep yourself alive.
There are prayers in your boots.
March.

Come home awake.

I will tell you a story.
You won't forget it. This is the job of writers.

Staying alive is the job of good soldiers.
And we know the dead are better soldiers.

This is not how the world needs you,
or anyone.
The world doesn't need any more sudden dead.
Even though you're good at it,
war
is just one side losing less.

# THE LONG, OUTSTANDING SALTATION INTO WILD OPEN AIR

**OKLAHOMA CITY, OKLAHOMA**
I stopped at Galileo's bar in the Paseo district.
Free beer if you are featuring your poems.
I can forget the whole show and know that the blur was beautiful.
Someone tried to sell me dirty DVDs in the parking lot.
One had the word "ass" in it three times and when that makes you laugh
it doesn't seem so dirty.
He didn't want to trade a poetry book for the movie.
Poetry will be worth more than lo-fi fake lust soon.
I remember making out once with a woman
in a handicap elevator around here.
Rowdy stumble-touch
is better than classy balance.
The night air here is flat.
The day is crème and crimson.
I know Dylan Thomas left a beer can onstage when he spoke at OU.
It was on display for years.
Someone stole that empty beer can.
Did they put it up to their ears like a seashell?
Middle American exit noise and dust bowl wrath poems.
Not worth more than
hand streaks
all over an elevator wall.


**NORMAN, OKLAHOMA**
My friends Beau and Jody are getting married today.
I got ordained online and agreed to pastor their wedding in the middle
of this cross country tour.
He has a lumberjack's beard
and a strong Springsteen half-sober face like a gunstock.
She has a white tinsel smile and jar of black olives for hair.
The ceremony was loose and real.
An older woman and I talked about snakes in the Bible and true love.

I danced with Beau's sister and threw her everywhere as
"Purple Rain" ripped open by good guitar drunkards
I remember a father, slow dancing earlier with his daughter.
I remember this the most.
Clumsy, gentle and unashamed.

He held her like he would miss her terribly.
When he let her go,
it was true and perfect.


### TULSA, OKLAHOMA
The moms here sure are attractive.
I heard Tulsa has a motel room where the Lord stays
when he visits America.
The thunder here is wide.
The people are holding out for holy.
The highways are coated in prayers and animals.


### PORTLAND, OREGON
Roller Derby, Roller Derby, Roller Derby!
Rain eats the walkers, the walkers eat the bikers
the bikers eat the cars, and the cars eat the shining streets, and the streets
eat the pine trees, and the trees eat the buildings,
and the buildings eat the nickel arcades, and only the bars are left
in the sweet drizzle.
The medics carry soup.
The churches have been taken over by artists.
No sermons. Music, bad lighting, art, poetry, and amateur cookies.
It is how church was meant to be.


### ANCHORAGE, ALASKA
Even the glaciers look desperate and royal.
Everyone here misses someone.
Come here if you are in love with
how things used to be.
You can feel far, even with friends around you.

A town becomes a gorgeous warning for shelter
when you realize that if you pass out
in a gutter,
you will be dead frozen by morning.


## COEUR D'ALENE, NORTH IDAHO

The cliffs lift sharp and green from the water like soldier's shoulders.
This lake is a coffee table mirror.
Not much happens here on purpose.
A house sits on the lakeshore with a woman fishing from the dock.
I hope the fella inside knows what he has.


## SHOSHONI, WYOMING

Pass the mellow hush of Powell
and all the curving river gorges of Thermopolis
to get to Shoshoni. The town is a sad song.
Don't you love them?
The Silver Sage bar smelled like stuffed raccoons and mop water.
The waitress told us they were closed.
She was as kind and as busy
as you could be in a town full of white dust and broken glass.
I feel at rest here. I feel this town settling in my mouth.
Across the street of abandoned shops,
someone spray painted a poem next to a drawing of Geronimo.
Beautiful words
and no one to read them.


## BOULDER, COLORADO

Lori Lee was a sweet kind of skinny, tan, flowing wheat kind of hair.
She was spilling with Shakespeare. He sure knew how to kill someone off.
Everyone in Boulder looked like a fitness coach or a hiking instructor.
Where are the gay bars?
We both didn't have much to say.
Paul Newman had just died.
The air crunches like snow that isn't cold.
Some people shouldn't die.

### DENVER, COLORADO
The Mercury Café is a chocolate éclair, dark, sweet and full of weird goo.
At some point during the show,
I threw some chairs to get at an audience member.
There sure are a lot of folks here with piercings.
They look like fish
that fought hard
and broke away from the line.

### OMAHA, NEBRASKA
It says the good life,
but it feels like the aftermath of Goliath's belly flop.
We met up with the fellas of Delta Spirit at a venue downtown
and danced our demons out. Jesse smiled and we danced on it,
dancing on that smile like the lights in the Billie Jean video.
You don't have to have beautiful
surroundings
to be surrounded by beauty.

### CHICAGO, ILLINOIS
Their bones are bright
and full with freezer burn.
The bicycles are drunk.
The lips of Chicago wrap around me in sausage skin.
The city is a heaving castle with asthma, rising from a lake that doesn't end.
Shoulders full of concrete and black ice, lift me up, lift me up.
Heaven's pub. Speak easy to me.
You laugh so hard in Chicago
your ribs rip and it feels like you're kissing
a dark-haired woman
in an elevator full of beetles.
Best people in the whole damn world.
18 degrees and still barbequing.

### DAYTON, OHIO

The Wright brothers are singing in the wind.
The university is full of black beauties.
Everyone gets lost in Ohio.
I dropped my virginity around here at 19 and
it reminds me that I want to tell my friend
who has a broken heart,
"Don't ruin love
by wanting it so bad."


### TRAVERSE CITY, MICHIGAN

Come see the opera house!
Come see the opera house dance floor where I split my pants
at the world's most gorgeous place for a poetry show!
Come see Michael Moore's sweat garden
and beautiful theater of cheap popcorn and starlit ceiling!
Come see the cherries placed into every object known to man!
Come watch the world blossom in a secret code.
Do not chop down the Cherry Trees.
Lie about it if you do.
Come prowl the stillness.
Come see the lake as it calls to the lovers
and come see the lovers answer
by walking into it, hand in hand,
and never returning.


### DETROIT, MICHIGAN

I used to see Detroit as a place that burns.
Detroit has pockets and they are filling with the machines of art.
You gotta let something burn to the ground
to build something new.


### SYRACUSE, NEW YORK

The nation's only horizontal traffic light
leads us to a tiny Irish pub. I spilled my beer on the floor
and we danced, slipped in the sawdust to some song
we would soon forget.

**PROVIDENCE, RHODE ISLAND**
There were so many pretty girls here,
I just went to bed.


**BANGOR, MAINE**
This isn't right. This just isn't right at all.
Cristin, her room across the hall,
with door open, called me and yelled into my phone
at the Bangor Motor Inn,
"I'm gonna murder you!"
Then she hung up.
I went to call her back,
but her phone was already ringing.
I knew she would answer it and think it was me.
It wasn't. She might have been embarrassed for how she answered
the phone. I soon called her back. I said,
"You're gonna get dead!"
She responded, "That's not right. That's not right at all.
We're all gonna be dead. Try again."


**ROYALTON, VERMONT**
We showed up to Mongo's ranch house in a tiny van
and we were covered in hot exhaust and cramps.
There was cold beer waiting and it wasn't bug season.
Do you know what that's like?
When you really want beer and it is already waiting for you
like a war bride, all cold and horny?
Vermont is the sweetest secret that should only be shared
when you have pancakes, cold beer
and orange red-matazz trees chucking its ticker tape
in its annual parade of maple privacy.


**JAMAICA PLAIN, MASSACHUSETTS**
There is a little white house aptly named, The White House,
full of musicians, artists, and writers.
We were to do a show there that night.
I spent the day at the huge pond, rowing a boat with some friends.

The swans swam in pairs. I slept somewhere alone.
I got a slab of ice cream that blew my mouth to shreds
at JP Licks and I don't even like ice cream.
I met a woman on the street while I was carrying my laundry.
She was a belly dancer. Weird how that happens.
You got a big burden
of smelly clothes
and someone offers to help you.
We chatted about wine, staying limber and other things I know little about.
We didn't get it on, but I sure felt good in her place.
The sepia tone show at The White House was in a little family room.
Perfect, no amp and packed.
There is a bag of chips with a retractable string in the living room.
You can pull it down from the chandelier
and offer it to someone and as they reach for it,
laugh as it zips back to its home.
I too want someone to tug on me with the smell of ocean
so I can zip back home.


### WALTHAM, MASSACHUSETTS
A tall woman with jet brown hair
had a laugh I dreamed of.
It was coming out of a carousel
and I just kept spinning, spinning,
reaching for gold.


### WHITE RIVER JUNCTION, VERMONT
This is one of my favorite towns in the world.
It is about as big as a slice of bologna.
Everyone here is bundled up and smart.
I need to open up a bar here.
Maybe it can be a library too.
I can't read when I'm tipsy
but maybe somebody can.

## HANOVER, NEW HAMPSHIRE

The leaves are changing like teak on a boat.
The students are wishing for warmth and it doesn't come.
The dorms are kissing chambers,
trembling in brains and expectations.
There is water when you enter this town
and a bridge
that makes you feel like you are flying into green laundry.
I could live here
if I was allowed to teach
all the words I have been trying to say
all this time.

## WEST LEBANON, NEW HAMPSHIRE

If you stop at the Four Aces Biker Bar,
you should get a bunch of breakfast.
If locals are looking at you,
they are just waiting for you to
introduce yourself.

## COLLEGE PARK, MARYLAND

Kenton, Gabi, Harry,
you are all I know of the good of this city
and you're from everywhere.
The stromboli is as big as your brave-guts.
Write your way back home.
Drinking and talking about the worst things we've ever done.
Julie was kind and too thoughtful to make that game forgettable.
Heather was doing pushups.
I think she was getting ready for Armageddon love,
her arms, sleek as solid snakes.

## NASHVILLE, TENNESSEE

In a drawl,
I missed you.

## FRANKLIN, TENNESSEE
There is a garden here
where over a thousand Civil War soldiers died
in hand-to-hand combat.
You can touch your fingers to the bullets embedded in the brick.
This is also a town known for having a large population
of contemporary Christian musicians.
So much blood in one spot.


## CONWAY, ARKANSAS
I remember a fight almost broke out at the pizza diner.
A dude from Texarkana, who came with a female reporter,
kept saying odd things; he was tired of liberals and faggots.
He was talking with Buddy.
Buddy is gay. He doesn't look gay to most folks.
Buddy is very buff.
Buddy was not afraid and offered to set him straight.
"Tell your family you got bowed down by a faggot."
The drunk dude and the kind reporter left before paying.
I think she was crying and I felt awful for her.
I felt great for Buddy. His eyes as wide as the Mississippi.
We found out later that the reporter
dropped the dude off with a few quarters at the gas station
a hundred miles from Texarkana and told him to find his own ride home.
She said he wouldn't stop yapping.
I didn't know her and I was so proud,
I had to write her down.


## ARLINGTON, TEXAS
The waitress at the Cracker Barrel Restaurant
thought we were in a band.
We told her we were writers and she gushed about her son
who was also an artist and made hip hop beats.
I can't remember his name,
but I remember her glowing like a bowl of halos
when she spoke her son's name.

## AUSTIN, TEXAS

There are clearly two lands called Texas.
There is the land of my father, in Cleveland, Humble, and Houston.
It is a land where you could blow up a car
and no one would care.
It is a land where we chased goats
and got chased by hornets and snapping turtles.
It is a hard land to be raised on
and I see it in my father's laugh lines.
Then there is Austin.
Prettiest women in the world: a liberal town with zero snootiness.
You can fall in love with someone, but for only four years.
Then, they graduate, leave and it is all understood suffering.
I remember drinking with the mayor once at a poetry show
and felt like the town had figured out endearment.
My father came to Austin to see the show,
ragged from the drive from Humble.
A woman was talking to him for too long so he got up
mid-conversation, kissed her on the cheek,
and walked to smoke one of his Salem cigarettes.
I thought that was a great way to excuse yourself.
I know he loves people, but maybe he isn't used to them.
I see myself in him as he stands alone at the back of the venue
watching me, watching himself.

## LLANO, TEXAS

Cows are in the front yard.
I have got to ride a cow today.
This town has a broken switch
that turns a dead town from slow to solid to perfect.
Depending on the elevation when you view it,
Llano is an Alamo waiting to happen.
Men sitting in the gas station
speak about who has the worst tractor problems.
Their cups of coffee last for hours.
You can do that when you are at
some kind of peace.

## Amarillo, Texas
There were wild horses.
There was your friend who just had a child.
Amarillo is where wind and babies meet,
so the children dress like kites, grow up and usually lift away.
At the Nat Ballroom, you can dance on the same stage that
Buddy Holly got hoarse on.
The road never ends. There is love in the barren.
The horizon is a train in quicksand.
We sold body tackles for a dollar.
This meant I would tackle you for a dollar.
We needed gas money. We were moving on.
Wild horses stomp and my spirit falls in love
with being alone.


## Truth Or Consequence, New Mexico
Near the Rio Grande, we pulled over at night.
The sky, gashed with stars,
only the high beams of truckers scooting beneath it.
Anis joked that this is what he usually saw during lovemaking.
It was so dark,
he ended up picking up a souvenir rock. He called it his
lucky rock.
I saw that he lifted it from the spot
I peed in when I got out of the van.
I wonder if he kept it?
I wonder if I should tell him?


## Hatch, New Mexico
Blood red chilies hung on the doors as year-long wreaths.
It is 93 degrees here on October 26th.
We ate at Sparky's BBQ.
Michelle stood behind the counter,
beautiful and far away, moving in the kitchen
like a youth pastor's wife.
It has been the same lemonade recipe for ten years.
The moose above our table seemed to be smiling.
I would like my head mounted with a confused

look on my face, looking back at the person I thought I knew,
now bringing me down for petty cash.
The sausage and ribs are glazed in secrets and butte powder.
The lemonade and you, they are your father's pride, Michelle.
Michelle, please get in the van.
The river is drying up.
The world awaits your sweet illumination.


## TUCSON, ARIZONA
There was a train moving behind the stage door,
every 15 minutes.
I wanted to open the backstage door
to just get on and go.
The people in the audience would have never
forgotten that show.
Short and sweet is better than long and convincing,
except during lovemaking.


## LONG BEACH, CALIFORNIA
The Prospector
Alex's Bar
The Queen Mary's Observation Bar
Joe Josts
The Dirty Bird, (Crow)
The Pike
The V Room
The Red Room
If you can hit all these places in one day
then you win the tournament of champions.
Tough to win because each place seduces you.
These are the places that put out the blaze.
Long Beach, I will be your unknown gutter laureate of 4th Street.
I will sing from the Gondolas of Naples
to the Merchant Marine staring out from Ocean Street.
He is waiting for the brothers who didn't make it to shore.
Long Beach, you are opening your arms.
Bring us your graduated broke, your sheared babes and floor peanuts,
your booze parade of labor, your renovated bones,

your shipyard ghost war.
You are spectacle in the sea of blue collars,
a gala of people hanging on
in unison.


### VENICE BEACH, CALIFORNIA
There is a small butterfly park
and the butterflies left the park to follow me,
zig-zagging as guide-ons down the sidewalk.
The nature
of mutual delight.
A crazed-looking man
got off his bike
to sing to a few pots of flowers.
Crazy has its dividends.
Great day in the history of great days.


### RENO, NEVADA
All you kids
left to rot here
are brighter
than all these casinos
smashed together.


### DONNER LAKE, CALIFORNIA
We jumped in
You shouldn't. Ever.
You will perish with a horrible look on your face.
Ice is supposed to be frozen.
This lake was a former harlot:
Beautiful on the outside
and ready to kill you
if you ever tried
to stay inside
her.

### SAN RAFAEL, CALIFORNIA
We invited the entire audience onto the stage.
We are all the show.
I laid on my back
and the words came out,
signals of smoke.
An audience
staring at the spot
of the small, steady fire
that I cannot extinguish,
that no one can.

### BERKELEY, CALIFORNIA
Bringing poetry to Berkeley
is like bringing a turkey
to a turkey farmer's house
for Thanksgiving.
Thank God that the farmer still tells you
that your turkey is the kind
she has been waiting for.

### COTTAGE GROVE, OREGON
I spent three nights here recording a poetry album,
at Richard Swift's house,
sleeping behind the controls.
I asked the brilliant fuzzy head of Richard
if he knew where he would hang his hat,
his final resting place.
He said, "Here, in Cottage Grove. We love it.
So many people come here and don't want to leave.
You start to love the rain."
Some souls never know
where they will plop down.
I envy those who can do the math.
The rain comes down, slow enough to see it somersault.
The Ax and Fiddle has good beer on tap
waiting for us as we stroll damp and ready for the night.
There is a small theater doing a play about a robot.

What more do you need?
We sit and I don't say much.
Jealousy does that to the tongue.

### BELLINGHAM, WASHINGTON
It is the last stop before Canada.
We sang songs at breakfast.
We sang songs at The Beaver.
A new president was elected tonight.
People ran through the streets with American flags,
most of them artsy-looking types.
I wonder if all those flags were just waiting in their closets
like their favorite coat
and everyone,
all at once,
was overwhelmed
with the welcome feeling
of new snow.

# Thank You

Thank you for the couches. For the stage light.
For the encouragement to keep at this kind of writing.
For the sudden make-out.
For the extra beer.
For buying a book when we both were broke.

# ABOUT THE AUTHOR

As one of the most original and well-traveled writer/performers in the country, Derrick Brown has gained a cult following for his poetry performances all over the U.S. and Europe. A poetic terrorism group has taken to tagging his metaphors across the globe. About.com called his former collection, *Scandalabra*, one of the best books of 2009.

To date, Brown has performed at over 1500 venues and universities internationally including The Tonight Show with Jay Leno, La Sorbonne in Paris, CBGB's in NYC, The Aquarium of The Pacific, All Tomorrows parties with the Flaming Lips and David Cross and a small Jewish youth group in Glendale. He is the president of Write Bloody Publishing so getting this book accepted was a breeze. He lives at sea in Long Beach, CA.

**brownpoetry.com**

# NEW WRITE BLOODY BOOKS FOR 2011

*Dear Future Boyfriend*
Cristin O'Keefe Aptowicz's debut collection of poetry tackles
love and heartbreak with no-nonsense honesty and wit.

*38 Bar Blues*
C. R. Avery's second book, loaded with bar-stool musicality and brass-knuckle poetry.

*Workin' Mime to Five*
Dick Richard is a fired cruise ship pantomimist. You too can learn
his secret, creative pantomime moves. Humor by Derrick Brown.

*Reasons to Leave the Slaughter*
Ben Clark's book of poetry revels in youthful discovery from the heartland
and the balance between beauty and brutality.

*Birthday Girl with Possum*
Brendan Constantine's second book of poetry examines the invisible lines
between wonder & disappointment, ecstasy & crime, savagery & innocence.

*Yesterday Won't Goodbye*
Boston gutter punk Brian Ellis releases his second book of poetry,
filled with unbridled energy and vitality.

*Write About an Empty Birdcage*
Debut collection of poetry from Elaina M. Ellis that flirts with loss,
reveres appetite, and unzips identity.

*These Are the Breaks*
Essays from one of hip-hops deftest public intellectuals, Idris Goodwin

*Bring Down the Chandeliers*
Tara Hardy, a working-class queer survivor of incest, turns sex,
trauma and forgiveness inside out in this collection of new poems.

*1,000 Black Umbrellas*
The first internationally released collection of poetry
by old school author Daniel McGinn.

*The Feather Room*
Anis Mojgani's second collection of poetry explores storytelling and
poetic form while traveling farther down the path of magic realism.

*Love in a Time of Robot Apocalypse*
Latino-American poet David Perez releases his first book
of incisive, arresting, and end-of-the-world-as-we-know-it poetry.

*The New Clean*
Jon Sands' poetry redefines what it means to laugh, cry, mop it up and start again.

*Sunset at the Temple of Olives*
Paul Suntup's unforgettable voice merges subversive surrealism
and vivid grief in this debut collection of poetry.

*Gentleman Practice*
Righteous Babe Records artist and 3-time International Poetry Champ
Buddy Wakefield spins a nonfiction tale of a relay race to the light.

*How to Seduce a White Boy in Ten Easy Steps*
Debut collection for feminist, biracial poet Laura Yes Yes
dazzles with its explorations into the politics and metaphysics of identity.

*Hot Teen Slut*
Cristin O'Keefe Aptowicz's second book recounts stories of
a virgin poet who spent a year writing for the porn business.

*Working Class Represent*
A young poet humorously balances an office job with the life
of a touring performance poet in Cristin O'Keefe Aptowicz's third book of poetry

*Oh, Terrible Youth*
Cristin O'Keefe Aptowicz's plump collection commiserates and celebrates
all the wonder, terror, banality and comedy that is the long journey to adulthood.

# OTHER WRITE BLOODY BOOKS (2003 - 2010)

*Great Balls of Flowers (2009)*
Steve Abee's poetry is accessible, insightful, hilarious, compelling,
upsetting, and inspiring. TNB Book of the Year.

*Everything Is Everything (2010)*
The latest collection from poet Cristin O'Keefe Aptowicz,
filled with crack squirrels, fat presidents, and el Chupacabra.

*Catacomb Confetti (2010)*
Inspired by nameless Parisian skulls in the catacombs of France,
Catacomb Confetti assures Joshua Boyd's poetic immortality.

*Born in the Year of the Butterfly Knife (2004)*
The Derrick Brown poetry collection that birthed Write Bloody Publishing.
Sincere, twisted, and violently romantic.

*I Love You Is Back (2006)*
A poetry collection by Derrick Brown.
"One moment tender, funny, or romantic, the next, visceral, ironic,
and revelatory—Here is the full chaos of life." (Janet Fitch, *White Oleander*)

*Scandalabra (2009)*
Former paratrooper Derrick Brown releases a stunning collection of poems written
at sea and in Nashville, TN. About.com's book of the year for poetry

*Don't Smell the Floss (2009)*
Award-winning writer Matty Byloos' first book of bizarre, absurd, and deliciously
perverse short stories puts your drunk uncle to shame.

*The Bones Below (2010)*
National Slam Champion Sierra DeMulder performs and teaches
with the release of her first book of hard-hitting, haunting poetry.

*The Constant Velocity of Trains (2008)*
The brain's left and right hemispheres collide in Lea Deschenes' Pushcart-Nominated
book of poetry about physics, relationships, and life's balancing acts.

*Heavy Lead Birdsong (2008)*
Award-winning academic poet Ryler Dustin releases his most
definitive collection of surreal love poetry.

*Uncontrolled Experiments in Freedom (2008)*
Boston underground art scene fixture Brian Ellis
becomes one of America's foremost narrative poetry performers.

*Ceremony for the Choking Ghost (2010)*
Slam legend Karen Finneyfrock's second book of poems ventures
into the humor and madness that surrounds familial loss.

*Pole Dancing to Gospel Hymns (2008)*
Andrea Gibson, a queer, award-winning poet who tours with Ani DiFranco,
releases a book of haunting, bold, nothing-but-the-truth ma'am poetry.

*City of Insomnia (2008)*
Victor D. Infante's noir-like exploration of unsentimental truth and poetic exorcism.

*The Last Time as We Are (2009)*
A new collection of poems from Taylor Mali, the author
of "What Teachers Make," the most forwarded poem in the world.

*In Search of Midnight: the Mike Mcgee Handbook of Awesome (2009)*
Slam's geek champion/class clown Mike McGee on his search for midnight
through hilarious prose, poetry, anecdotes, and how-to lists.

*Over the Anvil We Stretch (2008)*
2-time poetry slam champ Anis Mojgani's first collection: a Pushcart-Nominated
batch of backwood poetics, Southern myth, and rich imagery.

*Animal Ballistics (2009)*
Trading addiction and grief for empowerment and humor with her poetry,
Sarah Morgan does it best.

*Rise of the Trust Fall (2010)*
Award-winning feminist poet Mindy Nettifee
releases her second book of funny, daring, gorgeous, accessible poems.

*No More Poems About the Moon (2008)*
A pixilated, poetic and joyful view of a hyper-sexualized,
wholeheartedly confused, weird, and wild America with Michael Roberts.

*Miles of Hallelujah (2010)*
Slam poet/pop-culture enthusiast Rob "Ratpack Slim" Sturma
shows first collection of quirky, fantastic, romantic poetry.

*Spiking the Sucker Punch (2009)*
Nerd heartthrob, award-winning artist and performance poet,
Robbie Q. Telfer stabs your sensitive parts with his wit-dagger.

*Racing Hummingbirds (2010)*
Poet/performer Jeanann Verlee releases an award-winning book
of expertly crafted, startlingly honest, skin-kicking poems.

*Live for a Living (2007)*
Acclaimed performance poet Buddy Wakefield releases his second collection
about healing and charging into life face first.

# WRITE BLOODY ANTHOLOGIES

*The Elephant Engine High Dive Revival (2009)*
Our largest tour anthology ever! Features unpublished work by
Buddy Wakefield, Derrick Brown, Anis Mojgani and Shira Erlichman!

*The Good Things About America (2009)*
American poets team up with illustrators to recognize the beauty and wonder in our
nation. Various authors. Edited by Kevin Staniec and Derrick Brown

*Junkyard Ghost Revival (2008)*
Tour anthology of poets, teaming up for a journey of the US in a small van.
Heart-charging, socially active verse.

*The Last American Valentine:*
*Illustrated Poems To Seduce And Destroy (2008)*
Acclaimed authors including Jack Hirschman, Beau Sia, Jeffrey McDaniel,
Michael McClure, Mindy Nettifee and more. 24 authors and 12 illustrators
team up for a collection of non-sappy love poetry. Edited by Derrick Brown

*Learn Then Burn (2010)*
Exciting classroom-ready anthology for introducing new writers
to the powerful world of poetry. Edited by Tim Stafford and Derrick Brown.

*Learn Then Burn Teacher's Manual (2010)*
Turn key classroom-safe guide Tim Stafford and Molly Meacham
to accompany *Learn Then Burn*: A modern poetry anthology for the classroom.

*Knocking at the Door: Poems for Approaching the Other (2011)*
An exciting compilation of diverse authors that explores the concept of the Other
from all angles. Innovative writing from emerging and established poets.

**WWW.WRITEBLOODY.COM**

# Pull Your Books Up
# By Their Bootstraps

Write Bloody Publishing distributes and promotes great books of fiction, poetry and art every year. We are an independent press dedicated to quality literature and book design, with an office in Long Beach, CA.

Our employees are authors and artists so we call ourselves a family. Our design team comes from all over America: modern painters, photographers and rock album designers create book covers we're proud to be judged by.

We publish and promote 8-12 tour-savvy authors per year. We are grass-roots, D.I.Y., bootstrap believers. Pull up a good book and join the family. Support independent authors, artists and presses.

Visit us online:

WRITEBLOODY.COM